Kyle's War

Mario Milosevic

Green Snake
PUBLISHING

Kyle's War
by Mario Milosevic

ISBN: 978-1-949644-39-5

Published by Green Snake Publishing
www.greensnakepublishing.com

mariowrites.com

Book 1

Aunt Thelma says my mother wants me to fill up this notebook, only I've never written anything before except for school stuff and there are a lot of pages so I don't know if I can. But ok. I'll try. Should I tell you who I am first? My name is Kyle. I was named after my grandfather, who lives in Toronto, which is in Canada, but he used to live here in the United States. He was part of the government for a while, but then they kicked him out or he quit. I'm not sure which because I know about it from my mother, and she doesn't tell me a whole lot about him. That's mostly because she's mad at him for some of the things he did before he quit, but she won't tell me what those are so I can't tell you either.

The most important thing you need to know about me is that my parents are in jail. They'll be getting out soon, though, I'm sure of it, because they didn't do anything wrong. I guess I'm also supposed to tell you a little more about me. I live in this small town called Cedar Falls which is on the Columbia River where we have a dock and people from the sternwheelers and cruise ships stop here and come into town and spend money and that's how the town keeps going, according to my aunt Thelma, who is a real estate agent so she should know about that kind of thing since she goes all over the county showing people houses and convincing them to buy one. I go to school and stuff, but if I told you any of that you would find it boring because I think it is absolutely completely boring and it's my own life so whoever you are would find it ten times as boring I'm sure.

Cedar Falls is a dinky little town so you probably think I'm some kind of hick or something. I don't care. Maybe I am a hick. So what. I'm about fourteen years old. You don't have to know exactly. Plus, why should you believe me? Maybe I'm twelve. Maybe I'm sixteen. You don't know. I could also tell you I'm incredibly handsome and girls think I'm cute, plus I'm super strong and I'm the best at sports and I get straight As at school. Also I have X-ray vision and I can fly and just by thinking about things I can make them move around all over the place. Ha ha. OK, the last part no one would ever believe, but the first part maybe you believe. You don't know. I could be lying my head off and you would never know, so why bother about that? So I won't tell you about myself. Not completely.

Maybe a little bit later, if I keep writing here.

Our country is at war with China, which means boys like me will soon be putting on uniforms and grabbing guns and trying to kill Chinese people who will be trying to kill us, which is a pretty scary thing to think about, so I don't think about it too much. Also, it's not really a war, according to the people who are supposed to know about these things. Also, it isn't in China. The Chinese tried invading some countries in the middle east to get their oil, but we wouldn't let them, so now we're fighting them there. It is a contained conflict, whatever that means. I hear President Cooper say we should call it a cool war. She says it's not like a cold war, which is what we had a long time ago with Russia, and not like a hot war, which is what we had with Iraq, but something in between. My dad says that's just trying to change truth and reality with words, and it doesn't work. He's probably right. The way I see it, if someone's shooting at you and they're wearing a uniform, then that's a war. Calling it a cool war doesn't make it any better, in my opinion, which, since this is my journal, it's my opinion that counts. President Cooper says some crazy things sometimes, but then almost all grown-ups do, I've noticed.

Is that enough? I hope so, because I'm starting to run out

of ideas. My parents shouldn't be in jail, ok? That's the most important thing, more important than anything because they didn't do anything wrong.

It's my second day writing in this notebook. The first day wasn't so bad, except I wasn't going to do a second day or any other day because why bother? It's not going to change anything. But Aunt Thelma said I should. So here I am.

The mess all started when my mom and dad opened an art gallery. Don't ask me why they did this. Mom and Dad have some crazy ideas and they don't always figure out ahead of time what it will lead to. Not that they aren't smart. They are. But they sometimes do things, like the art gallery, that makes you think it wasn't such a good idea. On top of that, the art gallery wasn't even fun for them, as far as I could tell. They were always saying they didn't have enough money and the artists who paint the pictures are all so impressed with themselves, which I guess means they didn't like working with them. But being impressed with yourself isn't so bad if you really are impressive. But if you aren't impressive, then you shouldn't go on and on about yourself. My friend Lorraine is impressive, part of the time. The rest of the time, not so much.

All I'm saying is you have to match your talk and what you do to who you are exactly. Otherwise it's just all messed up.

And another thing about the art gallery. My parents spent so much of their time on it because they said it was their way to help save the world. Save the world. I sure didn't see how having a bunch of pictures on a wall was going to save the world. If you understand it, then maybe you could explain it to me some time. They would be at the gallery all day and they wouldn't come home until late and I would say what about me? What about saving me? And my mom would say you don't need saving Kyle. We're teaching you to be independent and have your own mind. I said you care more about art and stupid pictures than you do about me. And she said, that isn't so Kyle, but the situation in this country needs our attention. We need to question authority. You need to question authority, which is what she has been telling me forever, so I said, well you're the authority in this house and I'm questioning you. And then my dad said that's not what we mean Kyle, and I said, how am I supposed to know what Question Authority means? and why doesn't it mean questioning you? And then my mom said we're talking about the government and their intrusions. And then I said No, it's about you because you never change your mind about anything. You say the government is taking away our freedoms and we need to stand up to them, but all you do is show pictures and that isn't enough, I said, it just isn't enough, and besides that, how do I know the government is really doing something wrong? Maybe the government is just trying to protect us. Have you ever thought about that? And my mom made her eyes go real wide and she said, ok Kyle, if you don't want to question authority, then maybe what you want is to go along to get along and just Trust What Happens Next. I didn't say anything after that. I thought about what she said. Trust what happens next. It would be nice to do that, but you can't. Not really. Sometimes you can, but if you always trusted what happened next you'd probably be dead in no time.

OK. You're reading this, whoever you are. That is, if I don't burn it when I'm done. I haven't decided about that yet. I guess I have time for that. I guess no one's going to come into my aunt Thelma's house in the middle of the night and steal this stupid notebook since it's not like I'm some big important guy or anything. Except my aunt Thelma says I shouldn't say that because everything is possible now and I have to be careful. Everyone has to be careful. She's right too, because right after my parents got arrested the cops came to Aunt Thelma's house and searched it for a few hours looking for stuff that could make my parents look bad. They didn't find anything, though.

So anyway, everyone has to be careful. Even me. And not because I'm some kind of criminal or anything. In our town, at my school, I bet there aren't any criminals or terrorists at all. None. Not even that kid who drew a mustache on President Cooper's picture that was in the school library, the one with her pointing to us with the words underneath saying: IT'S RIGHT TO TURN IN DEVIANTS. The mustache was a joke, ok? There aren't any enemy sympathizers here either. None. And you can think the war is wrong without being an enemy of the country, ok? I don't want to be in any stupid war, but that doesn't mean I'm an enemy of the United States.

But anyway, no one in my school or in Cedar Falls is a traitor or a terrorist or anything, including my parents. You hear that? Neither are my parents. You didn't steal this hoping I would say they are, did you? If you did, you're wasting your time, so just give it back, jerk. Or leave it where you found it. The rest of you, I'll assume you aren't jerks and I gave this to you to read because maybe I like you or maybe I'm trying to get extra credit at school. Or maybe it's a hundred years from now and I'm dead and you're some historian who has to write a book about what was going on now, and you're trying to figure out what happened to my parents. In that case, it's ok. You can keep reading.

My mother says people used to question authority and that was an ok thing, but not anymore. In my patriotism class we learn all about how the people in charge are super smart and know way more than anyone else and we should always believe them. Right there that's wrong for the reason I already told you, which is that my parents shouldn't be in jail.

But anyway I've never written a journal before. I don't exactly know what to say here. Maybe I've done enough for today.

It's the next day. I guess I should tell you more about where I live. My town is called Cedar Falls because there are a lot of cedar trees here and because a long time ago there were some waterfalls on the river, but they disappeared when they built one of the big dams. So even though the falls are gone now, no one ever changed the name of the town.

I like to go into the woods and hunt around for mushrooms in the fall, or look at the flowers in the spring, or the colors of the leaves in the fall. Sometimes I get to see coyotes and elk and then I can stand there for a long time watching them. It's very cool. A couple of times I saw bears in the woods, but I wasn't scared. I made lots of noise and they turned around and ran away. That's what you're supposed to do if you don't want them to come up and eat you or anything. Bears do eat people sometimes. A couple of years ago some hunter was in the woods and a bear got a hold of his legs. Luckily the guy had his gun and shot the bear so even though he was hurt pretty bad, he still lived. I don't have a gun because I don't do any hunting, but I'm not scared of bears. You make enough noise and the bears leave you alone.

People who visit Cedar Falls are always asking where the falls are and people who live here have to tell them there are no falls anymore. It sounds kind of stupid. Well, it is kind of stupid. Anyway, that's where I live with my mom and dad in Washington state where it rains a lot in the winter but not too much in the summer.

Correction, that's where I used to live with my mom and dad. I'm writing this because of Mom. She told my aunt Thelma I should write in a diary. She called it a journal, which is pretty much the same thing only it sounds more official and fancy. My mother told Thelma if I write down my thoughts then maybe I'll get through this part of my life easier, the part where my parents are in jail for no reason. And I have to do it pretty much everyday for it to work. OK. I'll try. So far it doesn't make anything easier, but maybe it will after a while. Maybe. I don't know. She also said not to write it on the computer. They might be monitoring, she said. At least that's easy because my computer is at my house where I'm not living right now. But also, I remember once, before the whole journal thing, and before the art gallery weirdness, she said things on computers don't last. People might not be able to read stuff on a computer in the future.

At first I thought that was crazy. Computers are everywhere and everyone uses them. They must work, right? But then I thought about it some more and decided she was probably right. Not because she can see the future or because she has a time machine or anything. All I'm saying is Mom thinks things through. (Except for the art gallery mess.) Think about this: have you ever tried to load new software into an old computer? Get it? It's not going to work. Everything electronic turns into junk eventually. For example, how many people do you know who can play records? Hardly any, I bet, maybe none. So what happens when they stop making computers the way they make them now? That's right. All the stuff on computers becomes useless. So all I'm saying is Mom thinks about things. You might be thinking why don't I just print out my files from the computer if I want to keep them forever? But see, that just proves Mom's point because it's not on the computer anymore. It's on paper. Which is what I'm writing on right now, so why take an extra step and put it on the computer in the first place?

But anyway, Mom told Aunt Thelma that writing in a

journal is the old way of writing, and stuff that was written about a million years ago we can still read. Also you get to feel the power of true writing by using a pen on paper. I don't know what that means either so I'll have to think about it to really get it, but not now. Later.

My arm's getting tired from all this writing so I'll stop and write some more tomorrow.

OK it's the next day. My hand is all rested up. Aren't you hand? Yup. And you're all rested up too, aren't you arm? Yup. That's my hand and arm talking. Ha ha. They don't have much to say but I do so they'll just be quiet while I write.

Maybe I should tell you even more about me. I'm living with my aunt Thelma right now. I don't know how long it'll be because it's up to a bunch of judges and lawyers. They won't let me live at my real house because I'm too young, and guess what? My house is all trashed anyway because cops went into it looking for evidence about my mom and dad. So you might be thinking why can't they look for evidence without wrecking stuff in the house? I thought the same thing. I asked my aunt Thelma. She didn't know either. No one knows so you might as well stop wondering about it.

I just don't know how much to write here because I don't know who is reading this. But I'll tell you something you can count on that is no lie. My mom and dad are in jail because of some of the art they had in their gallery.

It's complicated, and maybe you don't care. That's ok. I'm going to keep writing about it, so it doesn't matter to me one way or the other. You don't have to keep reading. This next sentence is for people from right now, not to the future historians. If you don't care about what happened to my parents, that's cool because probably I don't care about you or your parents either and you can just go ahead and put the journal down and turn on your computer or the TV or the game box and become a vegetable if you want. Sautéed.

That's what my mother always says about people: they are becoming sautéed vegetables. When people ask her why she wants to run an art gallery she always says something like: We're trying to get people to stop being sautéed vegetables. Ha ha. I didn't get it at first, but Mom is like that. She says things I don't get. Then I ask her about it and she just smiles and lifts her eyebrows and looks all mysterious and stuff, like I'm supposed to figure it out on my own. That drives me crazy. Which she thinks is hilarious. But then sometimes after a while I think about it and then I get it. She's always trying to make me use my brain. That's what I've got to remember. It's like, people veg out when they watch TV, so if you come to Mom's art gallery you don't watch TV and you don't get your brains sautéed by the sex and violence and the commercials. Which, according to my father, is what TV is all about. He calls television the most efficient propaganda machine ever made. I had to go look up propaganda in the dictionary because my dad wouldn't tell me what it meant. I had to read the definition about a hundred and fifty times and I won't put it here because I don't want you to get too bored but basically it said propaganda is when you try to make other people think the way you want them to think. So TV is trying to make you think a certain way that you wouldn't even have ever thought of if there wasn't TV. Something like that. Which is a little bit crazy, you know, thinking TV is there to make you think. But I guess there are people around who are always trying to get you to think a certain way. President Cooper is like that. So are teachers. And billboards. And the posters at school about how killing Chinese soldiers is patriotic. If you think about it, that's almost all people do is try to get you to agree with them.

But see, my mom and dad, they're kind of different and they have different ideas. Even about art galleries. Maybe you think art galleries are full of pretty pictures, mountains and kittens and stuff. That's cool if that's what you like. That's sure what I always thought. Only no. That's not the whole story. My mom and dad put some pretty ugly paintings in their gallery. I mean disgusting ugly. I mean stuff you couldn't look at for even a second without feeling sick. That kind of ugly. Plus, a lot of the paintings were political, which doesn't only mean they were boring. Because, yeah, a lot of them were boring, but a lot of them weren't. For example, they had pictures of President Cooper torturing people. Yeah. It was ugly. She had these knives and hooks and stuff and there were other people in the pictures with cuts on them where the knives had gone into them and plus their fingernails were torn off completely and there were bamboo poles stuck in them and the paintings had blood everywhere and some of the people's guts were hanging out. The people had their mouths open, like they were screaming. Then, see, the people were yellow skinned, like they were from Japan or China maybe, which makes sense since we are at war with China right now, so that's the political part. But there's more because then on the floor, at the feet of the president were all these people wearing American flags and they were tied down and other people were taking the blood and the guts and forcing them down the throats of the people wearing the American flags. They were force feeding them is what my mother called it. Force feeding torture to the population. The population is us, the people who live in this country. And on top of all that the people who were getting gross stuff forced down their throats had big smiles on their faces like they were enjoying it.

So even if you never saw that painting, the way I described it is pretty accurate so I mean, come on, that was way disgusting and I'm not kidding. I brought my friend Lorraine in to see some of those paintings. There was a whole wall of them, a series where the president was doing different things in each picture and all the things were gross in one way or other. Lorraine said something when he saw them. He said shit, Kyle, you can't show this kind of stuff anymore. Your parents are going to get into all kinds of trouble for this.

So there you go. Even a dumb fourteen year old knew what was going to happen and my parents, who are supposed to be so smart, they didn't know. Not that Lorraine is dumb, it's just a saying. And in this case he was way smarter than my dumb parents, which is what I was trying to say. I guess that sounds like I'm mad at Mom and Dad. Well I am. Wouldn't you be? I mean the president torturing people? For one thing, it isn't even real. If there was any torturing going on, it wouldn't be the president doing it. So that's the first thing. And the second thing is, even if there was torturing going on, what is the point of putting it in a picture? Maybe there's a reason, but what is it? Back then I didn't know. Even now I don't know. And see, I didn't think Lorraine was right, either. I laughed at him. I said No way, man. No one's going to get into trouble. Not about paintings. I mean come off it. It's only pictures.

I guess the paintings were saying the president was a bad person and whoever painted them didn't like torture. All I can say is duh. Who likes torture? But then, why put it in a painting? I don't get it. And why the president? Maybe she's a bad person and maybe she isn't. I don't know. I see her on TV sometimes. Not at my house because we don't have TV. Because my dad thinks it's propaganda, remember? But where I'm living now, with my aunt Thelma, she has TV so I see it sometimes. Plus my friend Lorraine has TV and I used to go to his place. Oh yeah. I should tell you he's a guy even though his name is Lorraine. Yeah, he has a girl's name. So what? I told you he had some things to be impressed about. That's one of them. How many boys you know have a girl's name because they want one? His real name is Larry. But he likes Lorraine better. My mom says he's making a statement. I asked her what kind of statement? She said, He's your friend Kyle, don't you know? Well, no, I didn't know, and he wouldn't tell me. So in the end he's just my friend with a girl's name. Big deal.

While I'm at it, I guess I can tell you my mom is Alice and my dad is Richard. But if you looked at any TV or saw even the front page of a newspaper in the last week you pretty much know that. That's enough for today. My aunt Thelma says I need my sleep so it's time to close this diary. Journal.

Now I want to say some stuff about my parents so you get an idea about them. Once when I was at Lorraine's place I heard this crazy guy on TV, he was some politician running for office, and he said children should have the right to vote. Yeah. I'm serious. He said 7 years old isn't too young. He said as soon as a kid could hold a pencil they should be allowed to vote. I told my mom and dad about it, and I told them in a way they could tell I thought the guy was bonkers and they should think so too and besides that he was on television which makes your brains sautéed, remember, and then after I told them about him we would get a good laugh out of it, but that's not what happened. They looked all serious and they said it made sense to them for kids to vote because then maybe the people who ran for office would pay more attention to young people. They would maybe work for better schools and decent day care and health programs and other stuff that would help kids.

OK, I think my parents are cool and I love them and

everything and even though I'm mad at them right now because they're in jail which means I have to live with my aunt Thelma, for the most part I think they are pretty smart, even maybe about the smartest people around, but even though all that is true, I have to tell you that right then, I thought they were nuts because me personally, I should not vote in anything. Period. Not until I'm about thirty. Maybe forty. Really old, anyway. See, I don't know enough about anything. My vote would be an ignorant vote. And I don't care what anyone says, we shouldn't vote if we are ignorant. Because I've heard people say the reason we have such a bad president right now is because too many people voted for her who were stupid. I know what you're thinking: no one says the voters are stupid. You're right, they don't say stupid, but that's what they mean. They mean all those voters were ignorant, which is just another way of saying stupid. So if a lot of grown-ups are stupid about voting, then a lot of kids must be too. Maybe stupider. Definitely stupider.

But my father said, Kyle, if you had the power, maybe you would learn to use it responsibly. People in power have made decisions about other people during the history of this country and the world. People in charge have said this group is too young, or that group is too feeble minded, or another group is not the right race, or not male, and we tell them they can't vote. But that's an arbitrary thing. There's no natural law that says who can vote or who can't. It's a misuse of power to suppress others.

That stopped me right there, because I never knew that once only men could vote. Also I had to look up arbitrary which means something with no decision behind it, like when you roll a dice the number that comes up is arbitrary. I asked him if it was true about only men voting. He said it was completely true, which is pretty amazing to think about.

So maybe my parents were right about this. If the people who ran things once thought women shouldn't vote, then maybe the ones who said children shouldn't vote were just as wrong. I had to think about it, because maybe I could get smart enough if I knew the whole country was counting on me or something. But see, it wouldn't just be me. Everyone in my class would be allowed to vote. And they don't know any more than I do. Isn't that why we're in school? Because we don't know anything? Plus learning about who to vote for is like doing homework. You have to guess what they would do after they get elected and you have to do that by finding out all about them and what they did in the past in certain situations. It's complicated. Like homework. And I know how many kids in my class do their homework. About zero. OK a little more than zero, but not much more. And don't tell me you can just watch their commercials. You can't learn anything that way because they make the commercials themselves and they aren't going to put in anything that makes themselves look bad, I mean, come on. The internet is no better because it's lots different than it used to be. Dad said once the internet was completely free, but now the government makes sure all kinds of stuff never gets online. Or if it's there they have these filters that won't let you see it. You can only find stuff that says the government and President Cooper are about the best things ever in the history of the world.

So all I'm saying is learn stuff first, then vote. I figure if I stay in school and graduate, by that time I will learn about how to be an adult. There's all kinds of stuff to know about money and what food to buy when you go to the grocery store. Not just stuff you like but stuff you have to eat to be healthy and what things you have to be careful about doing so you don't end up in jail. Ha ha. Big joke, only not so funny right now. Anyway, you have to learn lots of stuff and voting is one of those. My parents are big on voting and I know they would say you have to be smart to vote. Correction, that is what I thought they would say until I mentioned about kids voting.

So then I made this expression I sometimes do where I lower my eyelids and tense up my forehead and my mouth and I nod real small, like I'm thinking and agreeing with them at the same time. They knew what that meant. I was getting way bored. But I didn't want to say that, so I was pretending to agree and also making like they were so smart and their point of view was too great to even think about disagreeing with. They ended up laughing at me and I laughed with them. So I'm telling you all this about my parents to prove to you that they are ok. They are not traitors or terrorists or anything. Far from it, ok? I know there are people who are against the country. But those are other people. Not my parents. With my parents it's just a big mistake. I think I should write it down a bunch of times, just so you get it through your skulls and into your brains. I'll be this voice in your head telling you the truth. My parents are not terrorists. My parents are not terrorists. My parents are not terrorists. My parents are not terrorists. My parents are not terrorists. My parents are not terrorists. My parents are not terrorists. My parents are not terrorists.

My parents are not terrorists. My parents are not terrorists. My parents are not terrorists. My parents are not terrorists. My parents are not terrorists.

That should do it. So if someone comes up to you and says Are Kyle's parents terrorists? you know what to answer back, right?

So now I will write about the president. I saw her on television today. I was sitting on the couch with my aunt Thelma. Cooper could let your parents out of jail right now, said Aunt Thelma, but she won't do it. She's drunk with power. My aunt Thelma doesn't like President Cooper. I know I have to be careful what I write here and everything, but it's ok if my aunt doesn't like the president. It doesn't mean anything. There's no one in the world who is liked by everyone. Come on. It's not possible. My aunt is one of those people who happens to not like the president. Big deal.

Aunt Thelma watches a lot of TV. She even has the TV on when she's in another room. Just leaves it on all day. I guess then she must have sautéed vegetables for brains, at least according to my mother. I never told Aunt Thelma what my mother said because she would think it was mean. If she wants to have the TV on, that's her business. It must be like her husband or something. Someone who talks to her in a way. I don't know. It's weird, anyway. She's never been married or had kids or anything. She had some cats once but she got tired of them and gave them away. They're very smelly, she said, and they shed like crazy. Aunt Thelma has the neatest house I've ever seen. There is not one speck of dust or dirt anywhere. She vacuums her place three times a week. Three times. I don't think we vacuum at our house three times a *year*. So that means I have to be extra careful when I'm at Aunt Thelma's to not be messy or anything. I can do that. It's not a lot of fun, but I can do it.

Aunt Thelma was right in a way. Mom and Dad *were* in jail because of the president. The president could just say, let them go, and the people who run the jails would have to let them go. They would *have* to because the president said so. That's how it works. But sometimes presidents do stupid things. They do. Don't even try to argue with me about that one, because it's just true. Now some other president who is maybe smarter would not make so *many* mistakes. Like my Mom. She'd be a cool president.

So anyway I was sitting there with Aunt Thelma and we were watching President Cooper give a speech on the draft law and how all young men and women had to obey the draft law. Especially young men because they were mostly the ones who shot the guns and dropped the bombs. What obeying the draft means is if they send you a letter that says you have to go to a war then you can't get out of it. She was going to come down hard on any unpatriotic teens who tried to get out of the draft. She was going to put them in jail for a long time and it wouldn't be an easy jail, either. It would be the kind of jail where they make you work hard and maybe you even end up dying real young because the work is so hard. Plus, they probably feed you crappy food and the guards beat you up. And when I heard the president mention the word jail, I had to wonder about what kind of jail my mom and dad were in. Was it the kind where they could die? Was the men's jail tougher than the women's jail or were they same? Were they getting beat up right now? I thought about that and I got all scared and sick inside. I just wanted them to come home. I figured everything would get straightened up in a few days and then they would come home. Only what was taking so long?

Aunt Thelma listened to the draft speech and then she put her finger on her tongue and made retching sounds as if she was upchucking. It was pretty funny watching my aunt Thelma do that because she's so neat and tidy and everything.

She would never no way ever in a million and a half years throw up all over her own couch, come on. Then after she pretend retched she said, No one should have to fight in any war if they don't want to.

I couldn't argue with that. Once my mom gave me a book that explained exactly what happens in war. It's not all glory and stuff. It's more about wounds and blood and people dying and they don't take care of you like they should if you're turned into a cripple without legs and arms. In fact, they almost want you to die because then it's cheaper for them than if you need all this medical care from getting your arm blown off or getting pieces of metal blasted into your face or having your guts fall out of you. So that's the first thing. It really hurts. It's pain you can't even imagine or make up. The book described the kinds of wounds people get who fight in wars. It was grosser than the pictures that got my mom and dad in trouble. You're probably thinking who doesn't know that when bullets and bombs are going off all around you then it's going to be pretty bad when one hits you, but reading it in the book made it more real. When they talk about war on TV it's always how great it is and how wars are so cool. Or that we have a duty to fight against the Chinese. But it's not like that. It's about the most horrible thing you could ever even make up.

And on top of all that once you've been in a war you end up crazy. Your brain is so warped you don't even know how to live with people who aren't soldiers. You get paranoid. You end up living on the sidewalks if you aren't careful. Plus you drink and do drugs a lot. It was all in the book. And I know you're going to say lots of soldiers come back from wars and they are fine, which is true, but a lot aren't fine and if you are a soldier you don't get to choose which one of those you are, the kind that goes crazy or the kind that is ok. See, that's the other thing, there are generals who make you go places where you will get shot and gassed and bombed. So yeah, I don't like the draft and I will get drafted in not even two years when I'm 16, so don't tell me I shouldn't have an opinion about something that could get me killed or make me insane. Don't even try. My mom gave me that book to read because she said everyone should have the knowledge to make decisions about their lives. The book said the government knows how to brainwash you into thinking the war and the draft are about the coolest things ever. Which is pretty scary right there. They use all kinds of things like school, the internet, magazines, and TV. Especially TV, which, I told you before is propaganda, remember? So this is a perfect example of how it works.

She has to let your parents out of jail, said Aunt Thelma. They weren't trying to do anything to the country. They were just selling disgusting art. That shouldn't be a crime. Aunt Thelma has some money from running the real estate office. I guess you can get pretty rich that way. She's been paying for lawyers for my mom and dad so I think she's pretty cool because that isn't something she has to do. Plus she doesn't charge me anything for food or rent while I live at her place. It's funny how she thinks about things. For example, she is mad at my parents, but she is mad at President Cooper too. She thinks my parents are stupid for what they did. But she thinks the president is bad for keeping them in jail. So how can it be both? How can my parents be wrong and the president be wrong too? About the same thing? I don't know. It's one of the things adults get but I just don't get at all.

See, Kyle, said Aunt Thelma, it's the way of the world. Cooper's making an example of Dick and Allie. She can't let them go because then people would say she's weak and she's putting us in jeopardy. But they only say that because she's a woman. A man wouldn't have this problem. If the president was a man right now your parents would be home. But Cooper can't do that. She has to make a show of them. It makes me sick, Kyle, it makes me so sick I could scream. If I could, I would take her neck in my hands and choke her to death.

That doesn't sound so good when I put it down on the page like that. But Aunt Thelma was just talking. That's all. So don't come after her or anything, ok? She's actually pretty cool.

My aunt Thelma said once I got going on this I probably wouldn't stop and she's right because I've been writing in here for an hour and a half pretty much non stop. So that's all for now.

February 12

Lorraine said I was like that guy with the mouse named Algernon. I said, who's that? He said there's a book called Flowers for Algernon about a guy and a mouse who get real smart then get stupid again. I said you think I'm stupid? He said no, except in the book the guy writes a journal. In fact the book *is* his journal. And I'm writing a journal so according to Lorraine I'm like that guy. I said ok. Then Lorraine told me I should put the date whenever I write in the journal and I said why and he said that's the way it's done so I put the date here. Just to make him happy. He also showed me his fingernails today because he painted them with pink nail polish and he asked me what do I think about it. That's something you don't see too often is a boy with painted nails but they looked kind of cool so I told him I liked them. He seemed happy about that. When Lorraine is happy I feel happy too. I guess that's what having a friend is all about. So I'm just saying: Thanks Lorraine for being my friend. Not that he's going to read this or anything. At least not yet. Maybe ever. Like I said I might just burn it when I'm done. Or put it in a shredder or something. Because so far I'm not sure it's worth anything at all.

I think it's time to tell you about the day they got my parents. It was about two weeks ago. I remember it was snowing outside. I was at the gallery after school doing my homework, which was some math problems from math class. There weren't any customers in the gallery. There were people, but they weren't buying any of the paintings. They were passengers from the cruise ship on the river that stops for a couple of hours and then the people go around town looking in shops and stuff and getting coffee and eating lunch and a lot of them come into the gallery. But mostly they don't buy anything. Galleries are like that. Even though the stuff is for sale, most people just come in and look around and then they walk away. It's like that all day. So you wonder how do you make a living from an art gallery. That's just it. You don't. Art isn't about making a living. It's about saving lives. That's what my mom says. She has this poster that says ART SAVES LIVES. See? It doesn't say ART BUYS GROCERIES or ART PAYS YOU WAY MORE THAN MINIMUM WAGE.

So anyhow, these three men walk in. Two of them are wearing police uniforms. The guy in the middle isn't wearing any uniform. He walks up to my mother and father. He shows them a piece of paper he pulls from his pocket. Then he says the gallery is shut down and they are under arrest for displaying artistic work that is counter to the public good, which is a violation of the federal decency and child protection code. My dad looks over at me. He looks so scared. My mother just looks mad and her face turns red. They don't move for about a millions years. I don't move either. My head is all thick and heavy. I can't breathe all of a sudden. Then my dad reaches for my mother. But the two guys in uniforms slap his hand away and turn my parents around and put handcuffs on them.

Then my mom starts screaming. What about my son? she says. Who's going to take care of my son? The guys who handcuffed her tell her to shut up. Call your aunt Thelma she says to me. She is screaming louder than anything. It is scary just listening to her. Kyle, call your aunt Thelma, she'll know what to do. She is screaming as loud as anyone can scream and she is kicking the guy who is trying to hold onto her. Don't let them put you anywhere else, Kyle. Call your aunt Thelma. Then the guy puts his hand over her mouth. I think she bites the guy's hand. I'm not sure but he yells and pulls his hand back, so I think she must have. My father is already gone. They dragged him out the door in nothing flat. I am so scared I don't know what to do. It's very embarrassing. I want to run up and hit the guy who is on my mother but I can't do it. I just stand there feeling stupid. The guy who got bit says the F word about three times. My mother says the F word too. She says F you you mother effer. F you. F off. She turns even redder and then she collapses on the floor and rolls over so her feet are up in the air and she is kicking at the guy. The guy tries grabbing her feet, but she won't stop kicking. He moves around to get at her head, but she spins around there on the floor and just keeps kicking. The guy looks very annoyed. Then another cop comes over. They get at either end of my mother and hold her down. She is still trying to kick at them, but they finally get her feet kind of clamped down on the floor and they ask her if she is going to cooperate and she yells at them to let go of her. So then another guy comes up and kicks her in the side. She folds up and wraps her arms around her knees and the guy kicks her again. Then the three of them get my mom up on her feet and she tries to slump down, but they hang onto her so her feet are dragging on the floor and they take her out the door and just like that my mom is gone.

Other people came into the gallery. They wore gloves and they took pictures with a big camera with a flash on it and then they started taking the paintings off the wall. They unrolled this thick yellow tape and hung it around the gallery. It had black letters on it. CRIME SCENE. My legs felt like they had turned into water. I was so sick. I wanted to throw up. For real. Some lady came up to me and put her hand around my shoulder. I jumped. She leaned close to me. She had on a police uniform. She smelled like something awful. Some strong perfume. She said something I didn't care about. All I could think was they hurt my mom and took my mom and dad. I tried to move but my legs wouldn't hold me up. I got dizzy and started to fall. The lady grabbed me. Don't be scared she said. I'm only here to help.

I didn't know what else to do except go with her. By this time there were about fifty people in the gallery. The lady said her name was Ellen something. They were going to take me to a place where they could help me and make everything better. But I knew she was lying. They took my parents and now everything was going to be different. Everything.

I know I'm supposed to write in here everyday, but when I wrote about my mom and dad getting arrested, it was too hard and I didn't want to write anymore. I mean, what is the point of feeling so bad? There isn't one. I already lived it when they got taken away so why should I go through it again in my imagination? If you want to find out about my parents then read the newspaper because they're there. Just about every day there's at least one article about them, usually more.

Ok, never mind, because everything in the newspaper is lies. I'm not kidding. I think newspapers must be propaganda machines just like TVs. They say Mom and Dad are leaders of some kind of terrorist group of people who want to kill President Cooper. Which is the craziest thing ever. They are trying to make people think a certain way about my parents and it isn't true. My mom and dad don't kill anything. They don't even eat anything other people kill. I'm not kidding. No fish or chicken or nothing. They don't even kill bugs. My dad takes bugs outside and lets them go. Yeah, stupid old bugs and he won't even step on one. So if they won't even kill a little bug, you think they would kill a person? Just think about it, whoever you are reading this. Just think about what it means that they don't kill anything.

Yesterday I asked my aunt Thelma when I could go visit my mom and dad. She said she's working on that. The lawyer she's paying money to is trying to arrange things so I can see them, but I'm not holding my breath because Aunt Thelma told me my mom and dad are not in jail just for showing bad art. The president decided the day after they were arrested that they were even worse than that. There's this law in the country that says a president can decide who is a terrorist and who isn't. It happened before when we were fighting Iraq. Only now we're fighting the Chinese but the law is still there so the president can use it any time she wants to, even if there is nothing to do with Iraq. Which there isn't, since that war is over. OK, not exactly over because I guess they are still fighting, but none of our soldiers are fighting there, so when I get drafted I'm not going to Iraq. I'm probably going to some place where China will attack us. But anyway, that's what the president did, she said my parents are considered terrorists so there are completely different rules for them now. Just for an example, no one can talk to them or see them. Aunt Thelma tells me all this and then my head just starts hurting because it means she never talked to my mother, like she said she did, and my mother never told her to have me write this journal. It was Aunt Thelma's idea of what she *thought* my mother would want.

And then she tells me we both have to be strong and then we can get through this. We should live as normal a life as possible. I think, is that supposed to be a joke? Because there's nothing normal about any of this. Then she told me Mom and Dad have had their rights violated, which means they haven't been allowed to do what they are supposed to be able to do according to the law. Except the president has this law that says she can do what she's doing, only the lawyer thinks the law shouldn't be there because it is against other laws. Or something. It's so complicated I don't get it at all. Aunt Thelma says the lawyer is working hard but I think he can't be working that hard if I can't even see my own parents yet. Plus, they are still in jail. I mean that's the big thing. They are still in jail. And oh yeah, MY PARENTS ARE NOT TERRORISTS. MY PARENTS ARE NOT TERRORISTS. MY PARENTS

ARE NOT TERRORISTS. That's just if you maybe forgot that MY PARENTS ARE NOT TERRORISTS. OK?

Now I'll tell you about what happened right after they got arrested. I went with this lady, this Ellen person, and we got in a car, and drove to this police station, which any other time would have been cool, but not this time. We went to a little room where Ellen sat me down and gave me a pop. Like I was supposed to think she was so nice and everything because she gave me a pop. I didn't drink it. I was shivering, so that meant I was cold, so I didn't need any pop. She asked me if I wanted a different flavor. I shook my head. I asked her where my parents were. Your parents are in serious trouble, she said, but we're going to take care of them and make them better, just like we are going to take care of you. We want everyone to be happy. Don't you want everyone to be happy? I said I guess so. She smiled big and said good, Kyle, that's real good. Now I'm going to ask you about your parents. Where are they? I said. Only she wouldn't answer me. She started asking me about who my parents knew and did I ever see anyone around the gallery who they were super friendly with.

I started telling her it was a gallery. People we didn't know come in all the time. It's like a store. No one knows who comes into a store because anyone can come into a store. She asked me if my parents ever ran meetings at the gallery. I said what kind of meetings? She said meetings where people talked about things. What kinds of things? I said. Art theory or politics, she said. Things like that. Maybe they talk about planning things. Events or other things. I said I never saw any meetings. She nodded and smiled and told me I was doing real well. She said I was going to be able to see my parents but she needed to talk to me first.

I thought about what my parents would do if they were in my situation. And it didn't take long to figure out they wouldn't say much to this Ellen person because if I said anything, then it might get my parents into trouble. So I started just saying I didn't understand and Ellen would ask the questions again in a different way and I still wouldn't answer and she would keep smiling but you could see the smiling was getting a little faked by now and then someone knocked on the door. Ellen said excuse me for a moment, Kyle, and then she opened the door and some guy in a police uniform was there. They talked for a while and then Ellen turned around and she looked mad, but she tried to smile real nice only it wasn't working and she went away and then Aunt Thelma came in with some guy in a suit.

That was the lawyer. I was so happy to see my aunt Thelma because I was sure she got everything taken care of and my parents weren't in jail anymore. But that wasn't it. My parents weren't out of jail or anything.

Oh Kyle, she said. I can't believe it. I called the gallery and there was no answer and I called your house and there was no answer, so I drove to the gallery and saw the mess. I was so scared. And look where they have you Kyle, Oh my god. Those stupid paintings. Aunt Thelma was crying. I never saw my aunt Thelma like that. She said she was taking me home. She meant her home, but I could tell by the way she said it that her house was also now my house.

February 16

Anyway, a lot happened after that. Everything was ordinary and everything was crazy and it was all at the same time. Aunt Thelma had a room she wasn't using so it became my room. She bought more food so I could go to the fridge any time I wanted and just take whatever I wanted to eat. I like those mini pizzas and I like turkey sandwiches so she got me mini pizzas and stuff to make turkey sandwiches. Except she bought real turkey and I had to tell her no, it had to be fake turkey because like I said we don't eat dead animals in our house and Aunt Thelma slapped her head and said, oh yeah. It was funny. I laughed. Then she laughed too and it was ordinary. But then it wasn't ordinary. It was all messed up because my parents were gone.

So we went to the grocery store together and I showed her the fake turkey stuff we eat. You could tell she didn't think much of it, but she bought it anyway. We bought other stuff too, then we came back to her house and after I was in my new room for a while my aunt Thelma called me to come eat dinner and she had some soup and some fake turkey sandwiches which was cool. We ate dinner, even though I didn't feel like eating. She gave me a journal. This one. Only there weren't any words in it, obviously. I talked to your mother today, she said. You saw her? I said. No, Kyle. They wouldn't let me see her, but they let me talk to her. On the phone. I thought, ok, that was something. Aunt Thelma said she told me to tell you everything was all right. She's being treated well and she says to tell you she loves you a lot.

And here I just started crying, you know. My mom tells me all the time she loves me and it never makes me cry, but this time it did even though she wasn't the one doing the telling. So Aunt Thelma started crying too. Then I remember she's my mother's sister so it makes sense she would feel bad too but we can't go through the whole dinner together crying so we blew our noses and we ended up laughing. A little. Actually, she laughed, but I didn't so much. I stopped crying, mostly, but I still felt bad.

Your mother wants you to keep a diary, said Aunt Thelma. She told me specifically. You should write in it whenever you want to but it's best if you write every day. Now right there

I thought I was getting homework. My mother was in jail but that didn't stop her from making sure I was doing my homework and learning stuff. So that was cool. I liked that. I told Aunt Thelma I never wrote a journal before. She said that's ok. It's a learning experience. By writing in it everyday you will come to understand yourself and the world a lot better. Your mother said it will help you get through this time while you are apart.

You have to remember this was early on and I was ready to believe everything Aunt Thelma told me. I mean, why not? She was my aunt and she wasn't going to do anything to hurt me, ok? She let me live in her house and even got food I liked. So don't think I'm stupid because I believed her. I know better now that she never talked to my mother. Because they didn't let anyone talk to my mother or my father. Not even the lawyer. That was one of the new rules that the president had, because it used to be that people could talk to their parents if their parents were in jail. Not anymore if they say you are a terrorist.

But Aunt Thelma was trying to help me. She pretended that she talked to my mother and she made it real by telling me just exactly what my mother would tell me to do. Aunt

Thelma knows that because she's her sister. So she was trying to make me feel better by making me do what my mother would have made me do. I know, it sounds terrible, like it is some propaganda thing where she's trying to make me think a certain way, but it's not the same. I can't explain it exactly, but it's not the same.

So I took the journal with the blank pages and I started writing in it. At first I wrote in it thinking I would just do it for a few days, until my parents came back. I thought all the police and judges and lawyers and all those people would figure out they made some huge mistake by taking my parents. Maybe they would make them stop showing those ugly pictures but that's all. Then my mom and dad would come home. I thought I just had to wait it out at Aunt Thelma's. I'm still waiting and waiting and waiting.

February 17

Lorraine asked me if I read that book about the mouse named Algernon. I said why would anyone read a book about a mouse? And then Lorraine said you read books for all kinds of reasons and not always for just the story. So I said where can I find that book? But I was thinking I was never going to read it. I'm already going to school and they give me homework. Plus, I'm writing in this journal so when will I ever get time to read another book? Lorraine said it used to be in the school library but now it isn't because the school took it out. It's on the list, he told me. I said what list?

He explained about a list of titles about two miles long which has all these books you aren't allowed to read so they can't be in schools or libraries or bookstores or anywhere. I didn't know about any kind of list like that. Most of the books on the list are considered subversive, or depressing, or contributing to morbid thoughts, or they have views counter to religious norms or they challenge the prevailing political paradigm or they are unpatriotic. That's what Lorraine said. He knows a lot of big words, more than I do and he can use them the way they are supposed to be used. I never heard morbid before but I guessed it meant things which made you depressed, like the paintings my parents showed. And then when I figured that out, I suddenly knew things I didn't know before. I knew what happened to my parents and what happened to the book about the mouse are the same thing. And not because my parents had pictures of a mouse in their gallery, and not because the book about the mouse had stuff about President Cooper torturing people. I don't mean the same that way. I mean putting a book on the list or putting my parents in jail is a way of suppressing things and people. It's the exact same thing.

Back at my aunt Thelma's house I asked her if she ever read that book about the guy and his mouse that got smart then got stupid again. She said she read it when she was a girl. It was called Flowers for Algernon. I told her Lorraine told me people couldn't read it anymore. Then she got kind of sad looking. And she said, They put that book on the list? That's awful. I saw a scrapbook on her table. It was open to some pictures of my mother and father when they were younger. She saw me looking and asked me if I wanted to go through the book together with her. I said sure. Then I saw her eyes were red and puffy. So I thought she must have been looking at the pictures and crying. I mean, you don't have to be some super smart detective to figure that out.

We sat on the couch and looked through the book. Aunt Thelma has a lot of pictures. She showed me when she and my mom were kids. There was one where they were in Halloween costumes. Aunt Thelma in a cat suit, with whiskers and a tail, and my mom looking like a pirate with an eye patch and a sword. That's how I got my nickname, said Aunt Thelma. I said I didn't know she had a nickname. Your mother always called me Cat after that Halloween, she said. There were pictures of my grandparents, too. They lived in Canada then. But then my grandfather got a fancy job in the United States and he moved down here, only my grandmother wouldn't move with him, so he went back home on weekends when he had time off from his job. He was some kind of professor of science and worked for the government. Aunt Thelma said he had a lot to do with planning stuff for the war with China, the warm war. I said I never knew that before. Oh yes, she said. Your grandfather was always very pro military. As long as I can remember. It's why your mother became such a radical. She's the younger one so it usually happens that way. I said, you mean she didn't like what granddad was doing in his job so that's why she has a stupid art gallery? It's a little more complicated than that, said Aunt Thelma, but I suppose that's right, in a way.

So I didn't say anything for a while but I was thinking maybe my mother was smart and everything but maybe she was a little bit crazy too. Because does it make any sense to hang up pictures of things just because you are mad at your father? Should I make some ugly pictures now because I'm mad at my mother? Think about it. The answer is no, obviously. But then also I thought my mother must know something I don't. Because don't forget my father is part of it too. He put up the paintings with my mother.

My aunt Thelma kept looking through the scrapbook. I saw pictures of my mother growing up. She had lots of friends in the pictures with her and there were some with my grandfather and they looked ok together. It didn't look like she hated him or anything, not that I could tell.

I flipped back and forth through the book. There was a picture of my dad and my mom together on a beach somewhere. They looked so young, like they were not much older than me. Which when I thought about it, made sense. I think they were still teenagers when they got married. My dad is American and my mom is Canadian. They ended up living in the United States after they got married because my dad had a job at a radio station. He lost that job when a lot of the radio stations were put out of business by the government. There weren't a lot of other people in the wedding pictures.

Then there was a picture of me. Not that you could tell, because I was this tiny thing and I was all wrapped up in blankets, but Aunt Thelma said it was me. Then she flipped through some more pages and there was a picture of my mother in a big march in Riverton. It was a picture from a newspaper. This was a few months after the attack by the Chinese, said Aunt Thelma. Your mother was very brave. She went on the streets and protested what the government was doing, how they were ramping up to a war so quickly. That was also about the time your grandfather took that job. Then everything went downhill. It wasn't long before we found out he was doing some awful things, figuring out how to hurt people. So your mother and your grandfather had a falling out.

Oh, I said. Was there a riot or anything when she went on the march? Aunt Thelma shook her head. People got hurt when the police moved in. That was when everything changed.

It was bad before then, but it just got a lot worse. That's when the curfews went in and they started cracking down on free expression.

My aunt Thelma got this shake in her voice and I started feeling embarrassed again because I pretty much knew she was going to start crying soon. So I said maybe we should put the album away for a while. It was to try to make her feel better, but also I started feeling a little bit sick again because after seeing all those pictures I thought, this is it. I'm never going to see my parents again. I'm just going to see them in some dumb photo album for the rest of my life.

February 20

I asked my aunt if she wanted to read my journal. She didn't answer me at first. So I asked her again. She looked around like I wasn't even in the room. I saw a bottle of wine next to her and it was almost empty so I knew why she was a bit spacey. I went and got a blanket and put it on her. She was stretched out on the couch. I guess she was pretty sad about my mom and all. Her sister. She was happy for the blanket. She pulled it up around her chin and closed her eyes. Pretty soon she was sleeping. I didn't leave her alone. Mostly because *I* didn't want to be alone. The house was so empty and quiet. Aunt Thelma's house is never quiet because of the TV on all the time, but this time the TV wasn't on, so it was super quiet.

I sat down on the other end of the couch and I took the album and looked at pictures of me when I was a kid. Some of the pictures I don't even remember being where the pictures show I was. I was a real skinny kid. I had blond hair, only now

I have darker hair. And I had big feet. There was a picture of me and my grandfather. We stood next to each other on a driveway. I remembered that picture. Aunt Thelma took it. It was only a few years ago when my grandfather was back living in Canada. I was about ten. He came down to visit for a while, but he didn't stay long. He and my mom got in a big fight about something and he went outside and slammed the door and drove away. But the day before that, we stood outside and Aunt Thelma took our picture.

In the back of the album I found some pictures of Aunt Thelma beside a painting on an easel. She was holding a brush and was just about to put the brush on the picture. I thought, huh, my aunt Thelma is an artist. But she doesn't do that anymore, as far as I knew. What she does now is sell houses to people which mostly means she drives around a lot. Then I looked at the picture closer and she looked much younger than she is now. So she used to be an artist or something and now she wasn't. I wondered if that's why she didn't like the pictures in my parent's gallery. Maybe she knew more about art and could tell they weren't that good as far as pictures went. Her painting was not ugly or anything. It was trees and birds. Nature stuff. It was nice because it was the kind of thing I see when I go hiking in the woods.

So after I went through the scrapbook I tiptoed away from Aunt Thelma and went to the kitchen and called Lorraine to see what he was doing. His mother answered the phone. Oh, she said, it's you Kyle. Yeah it's me I said. Can I talk to Larry? Larry is very busy, she said. He's going to be very busy for a long time so I think it would be better if you didn't call him anymore. Lorraine wouldn't be too busy to talk to me. That didn't make sense. For one thing, I only ever talk on the phone for about three minutes. For another thing Lorraine is not a busy guy. He doesn't play sports or do any school clubs or anything. He pretty much reads and watches TV. So right away I knew his mother was lying. Well, maybe not lying, but something was wrong. Can you tell him I called? I said. No, Kyle, I don't think so. Please understand. We don't have anything against you, but your parents have put us all in danger. Just please don't call here anymore. And then she hung up.

The thing is, Lorraine gave me a copy of Flowers for Algernon. It wasn't the real book. It was a photocopy. He said it was dangerous for him to be giving me the book, but he wanted me to read it and there wasn't any other way to get it. So the photocopy was old and the print was gray and faded. The pages were all worn out. It looked like some kind of antique. I asked him where he got it. He told me there are people who have copies like this and they lend them out to anyone who wants to read them. But Kyle, he said, you can't tell anyone about them because if the government finds out, then those people would be in serious trouble, like your parents.

So I told him thanks. He said be very very careful with this and give it back when you are finished reading it. I read the first few pages. It was funny reading a book on big pages like that. I had to hold them sideways because whoever photocopied them put the pages side by side so there are actually two pages per page. I guess maybe that saved paper or something. But anyway, I just wanted to tell Lorraine thanks for the book and so far I was liking it. It looked like I was going to have to talk to him in school because his mother didn't let me talk to him on the phone. Probably she didn't understand I had nothing to do with those pictures in my parent's gallery. I mean, come on. Anyone should know that. I'll tell Lorraine tomorrow and everything will be ok.

February 21

A lot happened today. My grandfather called. Aunt Thelma went out with a man. And Lorraine said he couldn't be my friend anymore.

In fact my aunt Thelma is still out. I'm awake writing in this journal. I don't sleep much since they got my parents, so when I can't sleep I write in this diary. It's not my fault. My aunt says she has some sleeping pills if I want them. It's not like she's making me take them or anything. She just says if I want them then they are there. So far I don't want them. If I can't sleep then I can't sleep. It's no big deal.

My grandfather called early in the morning. Aunt Thelma answered the phone and they talked for a while. Mostly about my mother and father. Aunt Thelma kept saying no Dad, there's nothing anyone can do. Thanks for offering. Stuff like that. She said I know we have to be careful what we say. I know they're monitoring. It was a strange phone call because Aunt Thelma did not sound like herself. Not at all. It was more like she was a copy of Aunt Thelma who looked the same but had a completely different voice. Like a robot voice.

They talked for a while and then she handed me the phone. He wants to talk to you, she said. It was only about three minutes before I had to go to school but I took the phone anyway and said Hi. Hello Kyle, he said. How are you holding up under these unfortunate circumstances? I'm ok, I said. He said, It sounds like your aunt Thelma is doing the best she can. I want you to know that I'm thinking of you and if you ever need to talk to anyone, anytime, you can call me. OK? I thought, yeah I can call you in Toronto, but so what? What is he going to do from Toronto?

I said ok, even though I think I will probably never ever call him but that is not the sort of thing you tell people on the phone. Even I know that. It's called being polite. People say lies like that all the time, only it's not really lies. It's just what people say. So then my grandfather said, Hope you have a good day in school and then he said bye and I said bye and we both hung up. Aunt Thelma took the phone to put back. He can be a sweet man, she said. I'm glad he called. Yeah I said, only I could tell she wasn't all that thrilled that he called. It's more politeness. He got sweeter after Mom divorced him said

Aunt Thelma. Only I'm not ready to be sweet to him again. At least not yet. She said it like she was talking about something she didn't like to eat. My grandmother I've never seen. My mother told me she's in New Zealand. I always thought it was crazy that someone would move so far away.

So anyway I went to school and it was pretty boring. Since I was reading the Algernon book when I wasn't in school, I could tell that school was a lot different than it had to be. We always read boring stuff in school about how everyone should be super patriotic and never criticize things because there are smarter people than you running things. Which, right there, just isn't true. I mean sometimes it's true, but it isn't true all the time because if the smart people knew how to run things then there would never be disagreements, and the people who run things are always disagreeing, so how can they all be super smart but they don't have the same ideas about things? Just think about that, ok. They can't all be smart, and all think opposite things.

So yeah, school was boring boring boring. But I went and sat down beside Lorraine at lunch time like I usually do and he was not the same at all. How you coming along with that book, he said. I'm not finished reading it, I said. That's right, he said, you're kind of a slow reader. I forgot. Listen Kyle, he said, my mom says I can't be your friend anymore so we can't talk to each other out in the open. But I didn't have anything to do with the art, I said. Tell your mother that. Lorraine said it didn't matter. She had made up her mind so we were going to have to pretend to not be friends for a while. I didn't like that but I said ok. Then he grabbed his tray and walked away like he was real mad, stomping his feet real loud. I was alone at the table and other kids were looking at me like maybe there was something wrong with me. I ate my lunch. It felt pretty bad, even though I knew Lorraine was putting on an act. Then the rest of the day at school no one would talk to me or look at me or anything. I knew why. It was because almost everyone liked Lorraine and if he didn't want to be seen with me then no one else would want to hang around me.

I have more to tell about today but I just don't feel like it anymore. I also don't want to be writing in this stupid journal anymore. Maybe never again.

February 22

OK I lied. I'm writing here again. But ha ha it's going to be really really really short.

February 23

Don't blame me. It's my hand. It wants to write here. I can't stop it. Stop stop, hand. Stop. Ha ha. Big joke. Who cares.

February 26

Lorraine is talking to me again, only in secret. He doesn't want his mother to find out because she would be beyond mad at him he said. His mother would kill him. Not really, but you know what I mean. It's just something people say.

On those days when I wasn't writing here I went hiking and read Flowers for Algernon in the woods. It was about the saddest book ever. In the book they make a super smart mouse with a scientific experiment and then they figure out how to make the guy who is writing the journal smart the same way, because that guy starts out very stupid. So he becomes about the smartest guy in the whole world ever, but then he figures out that what made the mouse smart only lasts for a short time, so it will only be a short time for him too and then he gets stupid again. Plus, the mouse dies and that means the guy's going to die too. That was a sad book. But in a funny way I'm glad I read it. Because I could see why the school wouldn't want us to read a book like that. I mean, come on. It's a completely sad ending. Nothing good in it at all. But then, you have to think about this: does it tell the truth?

That's what Lorraine said when I gave the book back to him. He asked me what I thought of it. We were under the stairs at school and we were whispering so no one would hear us. I told him it was sad. I know it's sad, he said, but did it feel true to you? I said of course it's not the truth because whoever wrote it just made it up because there's no such thing as something that can make you super smart practically overnight so it can't be the truth. But he said don't so sure, Kyle. There are many scientists who can do amazing things and make brains do amazing things. And anyway, I'm not talking about literal truth, Kyle. What I'm asking is did the book feel true? Which I thought was a stupid question because if something is true or not has nothing to do with what it feels like. Is it true or isn't it? But then we had to go to patriot class so we didn't talk about the book anymore. I wanted to talk some more but I was just glad Lorraine was still my friend, even though we had to be secret about it.

Oh yeah. My mother is in the hospital. I mentioned that before. My aunt Thelma said her appendix burst. I didn't know that could happen. But it does happen to people and then they have to go get it taken care of in a hospital or they could die. So I said she isn't going to die is she? and my aunt said no no Kyle. She's going to be ok. But really, it doesn't matter if she's in the prison or at the hospital, because either way I can't go see her. Aunt Thelma said they have about fifty guards around her room and even though the lawyer tried to get them to let us go see her it was no way José, are you kidding? Dream on. And all like that. So my mom is in the hospital. And I hope you know I know there aren't really 50 guards at her room. I'm just saying they are guarding her pretty good, that's all.

Plus, the lawyer told Aunt Thelma the state department said she isn't allowed to leave the country. Yeah. They made her passport into a useless little booklet is the way Aunt Thelma said it. She has to stay in this country and so do I because there are members of our family who are under suspicion of being terrorists. Aunt Thelma said she wasn't planning to go anywhere, but it made her mad that they could just make her stay. I already figured out that if they can put my parents in jail, then they can do just about anything they want to do. I've said this before, but I'll say it again. MY PARENTS ARE NOT TERRORISTS. Maybe I should get a big piece of paper and make a poster that says that. Maybe then the lawyers and police and all those people will get the idea.

Oh yeah, and my aunt Thelma went out with a guy. They went to dinner at some restaurant in Riverton, which is the big city about half an hour from Cedar Falls. Then after that they went to a theater where they sing opera, which I have heard opera and I don't get why anyone would go listen to it. Maybe it's something you learn about when you are a grown-up.

I saw the guy before they went out. His name is Les. My aunt Thelma said he works as a security guard at a mall in Riverton. Aunt Thelma thinks he's funny because sometimes he acts like he's a real cop or something, but he isn't. Which is ok if you ask me. I would like it better if my aunt Thelma hangs around with a fake cop instead of a real cop, since real cops put my parents in jail. Les is tall and he had on a nice suit. Aunt Thelma had a fancy dress. She looked very different from on other nights. It was like she was a princess from a story book or something. She told me they would be out late but I was old enough to be on my own and if I needed anything or something happened I could just call the neighbors. I said ok. They didn't get back until after I fell asleep. I was asleep on the couch with this journal next to me. Aunt Thelma shook my shoulder and I got up and went into my room. I felt lonely.

I missed my mother and father. I was starting to get worried that maybe things weren't going to turn out ok. Maybe it isn't just in made up books that sad endings happen.

Guess what. I'm kicked out of school. Yeah. No more homework. Ha ha. Only it's not funny. It's pretty serious. What happened was Lorraine and I were sitting on the steps outside school and this jerk kid walks by and says, Hello fags how's your fag meeting coming along? Now usually the thing to do about jerks like that is you pretend they don't even exist and then they usually go away. Everyone knows that. I know that. Lorraine knows that. Only this time I guess Lorraine wasn't in the mood to ignore jerks. Instead he stood up and told the guy to F off and go screw himself. So this other kid didn't like that. He said What did you say to me you F-ing fag and Lorraine says you heard me and then the guy says he doesn't take orders from asshole fags and then he called me a fag too, like that was some awful thing or something. I stood up next to Lorraine who told the guy to go F himself. The guy just laughed and then he said Correction, you aren't a fag Kyle. Now don't get me wrong, your friend Lorraine here is definitely of the faggish persuasion, but you, you're not a fag, you're an F-ing traitor just like your F-ing terrorist traitor parents who will be tortured and hung like they deserve.

Then I got hot all over, like my head was going to completely come apart into a million pieces because there was this balloon inside of it and it was getting bigger real real fast. The kid laughed at me. Yeah, yeah, he said, especially your mother. She's going to be tortured the worst. They're going to take all her clothes off and cut her up bad and then torture her for days.

Lorraine put his hand on my shoulder to make me turn around so we could just walk away from this guy, but that isn't what happened. Instead I ran right at the guy and jumped on him and just started hitting him over and over again. That's what it felt like, anyway, but really I think I only hit him twice. Once pretty hard so my hand hurt, and the other time not so much. Then we both fell to the ground and I couldn't hit him anymore. I made my arms try to hit him but I couldn't move them that good when I was on the ground, and the guy rolled over and then he was on top of me and I couldn't push him off and I thought, oh no, I'm going to get hit pretty bad, but he just sat on me and held my arms and stared down at me.

He was all red and we were both breathing hard. Then he said think you're tough traitor fag? Huh? Think you're tough?

It wasn't like he wanted me to answer or anything, he was just being a stupid jerk. So I didn't answer him. But I'll answer here so you can read it that I'm not tough. I'm just not. I never get into fights except for this one time because I just couldn't help myself. So I didn't say anything, and I was still trying to get my arms loose, but he had too good a grip on them and I couldn't move them hardly at all. Then he purposely dropped a huge gob of his spit on me, which was too gross. It fell on my nose and slid down to my mouth, which I tried to keep closed so the spit wouldn't get inside.

Then Lorraine came over and grabbed the jerk from behind by his shirt and pulled him off me. The jerk looked way surprised, like he never expected something like that, and he fell to the ground, but he wasn't scared or anything. He was laughing, like this was all some big joke. By this time there were other kids watching. Lorraine and the jerk wrestled on the ground and after I wiped the spit off my face I went over and tried to grab his arm so I could pull him off Lorraine who was starting to get crushed under him. Then some teachers come running up and the next thing we know, we were all in the vice-principal's office and he was about as mad as anyone can be.

The jerk who dropped his spit on me said he was just walking by and said hi to Lorraine and me, and then I started hitting him. He had a big bruise on his forehead which is where I hit him. When I look at the bruise, my hand starts hurting again and I think, what was I thinking doing that? Am I the stupidest kid ever in the history of the world? The vice-principal let him go and the guy grinned real wide and kind of danced out of the office and then the vice-principal looked at Lorraine and me and he shook his head. Why is it necessary for the two of you to gang up on someone like him? he said. Lorraine didn't say a thing. Not one word. Nothing to say? said the vice-principal. I was all ready to tell the vice-principal everything. About how the other kid was calling us names and he wasn't leaving us alone, but then, see, it was me who actually started the fight. I mean, sure the other kid was being a jerk, but when you look at the facts I was the one who attacked him. I didn't want to, even though I did. It's hard to explain, but when he talked about my mother. That's what did it.

Miss Husum said you both ganged up on him, said the

vice-principal. Why did you do that? What's wrong with the two of you? Lorraine was still saying not one word, so I didn't say one word either. Larry? said the vice-principal. Anything to say? Lorraine was like a statue. The vice-principal sat there like he was thinking things over. I must also say that some of your behavior lately has us worried, he said. Painting your fingernails pink. Is that really something you want to be doing? Lorraine didn't answer. I understand you like to go by a girl's name, is that true? Lorraine still didn't answer. The vice-principal sighed. You don't have to talk to me if you don't want to, he said, but if you don't then it could go much worse for you. Is that what you want? Lorraine said nothing. Total silence. He was completely impressive, I have to tell you. Fine, said the vice-principal. Have it your way. Then he looked at me. Now Kyle, he says, you've been through a lot with your parents getting caught and so on, but that's no excuse to be going after other kids. Understand? I nodded. If you concentrate more on your studies, then everything would be fine. I want you both to be on your best behavior from now on. I think to myself, that sounds pretty good, he's going to let us go. But then he said, Kyle, it has come to my attention that you have been reading a forbidden book. Is that true?

Then I got panicky. My head started thumping again and I looked over at Lorraine, who still had not moved an inch. It's pretty amazing how he just sat there the whole time. I didn't say anything, but the vice-principal said, Never mind, you don't have to answer. I can tell by your reaction that it's true. What we want to know from you is where did you get the book? And before you answer, I want you to consider the fact that I could suspend you from school, which would be a very bad thing, because as you may or may not know, the better your school record, the more likely you would be to get a favorable and less dangerous assignment when you get drafted. Or I could decide to give you another chance and not suspend you. It's up to you. So I'll ask you again, where did you get that forbidden book?

So maybe you are wondering if I would tell on Lorraine. Do you really think I would do that? If I told the vice-principal about the book then Lorraine would be in trouble. So the answer is no way, I didn't tell where I got the book. But don't think it was easy. It was hard, because I didn't know that about the draft and I thought maybe he's making that up but maybe he isn't and I sure didn't want to get into any dangerous places when I was drafted. Well, who would, right? But even though

I thought about all that, I didn't tell. I said I found the book. Oh, said the vice-principal. You found it. Where did you find it? I told him I found it outside. He said where outside. I said I didn't remember, maybe over by the fence by the baseball diamond. He said, I don't believe you Kyle. Are you going to tell me the truth? So I just said I found it. I didn't know what else to say. Then the vice-principal shook his head again. OK, he said. Have it your way. Larry, you are suspended for three days for fighting in school. Kyle, you are also suspended for three days for fighting in school, and another three days for reading forbidden books. Then he sent us into the room outside his office where some secretary called Lorraine's parents to come get him and called my aunt Thelma to come get me. And now I'm back home writing in this journal and I still don't get what happened. Some jerk calls us names and then we end up in trouble. It's just weird is what it is.

February 28

I was worried that my aunt was going to be mad but she wasn't. Not at all. I told her the whole thing and she just listened and then she said there was no reason for that boy to taunt you like that. And for him to spit on you, that's terrible. Why didn't you tell the vice-principal what really happened? It was a good question, that's for sure, because I didn't know why, except Lorraine wasn't saying anything, so I wasn't going to say anything either. Plus, no matter what, you don't tell on other kids. Don't ask me why, because I'm sure my mother would say I need to think that through a little more, but I'm tired of thinking about things for a while. And maybe some things are the way they are because they're supposed to be that way. I know. That doesn't make any sense. All I'm saying is I'm tired of thinking about things, that's all.

So I told my aunt Thelma I don't know why I didn't do any of that. And then she didn't ask me about it anymore, mostly because she was going on a date again with Les. This time they were going to go to 3 or 4 different art galleries that were all having opening shows that night in Riverton. So she was happy about that and didn't want to pay much attention to me. So later Les showed up at the house and he was real interested in me. He said hello Kyle, and then he gave me a fancy pen. It had a ribbon around it, I guess to make it seem like it was a present or something. Only I looked a little more close and it was not really a fancy pen at all. It was just some cheap plastic pen that he put a ribbon around. Big deal. I can get a pen like that anywhere. And it wouldn't have a stupid ribbon on it. He said your aunt Thelma tells me you keep a journal. I think that's marvelous so I thought you might like a nice pen to write in it. So I took the pen and I felt embarrassed, because for one thing, what was Aunt Thelma doing telling Les I wrote in a journal? And then for another thing I could tell right away I wasn't going to like the pen because it was too thick and just didn't feel right. It was completely unbalanced, heavy at the top and light at the bottom. But Les was Aunt Thelma's friend and I know you don't say anything bad when someone gives you a present so I said thanks. Aunt Thelma got the widest smile I've ever seen on anyone. I thought maybe Aunt Thelma would like the pen more than me and I'll give it to her later, but I didn't say anything right then. I just kept quiet about it. That's usually the best way to go. It's way safer than saying something stupid or something that will get you into big trouble.

So now they're gone on their date and normally I would call Lorraine and talk to him but I can't do that anymore because of his mom so I guess I'll just

March 1

OK. I didn't finish that last sentence last night because as I was writing it the doorbell rang and guess who it was? It was Lorraine. I was so surprised to see him because I was sure his parents weren't going to let him out of the house. I was right about that. He said everything's different now Kyle. I had to sneak out of the house to come here because my parents are freaked about my suspension. I've *really* got to get away from this town. And by the way, thanks for not telling about the book, because then I would have been in even bigger shit if that's even possible. I said no problem, and he asked me if I was doing anything tonight and I said no but my aunt Thelma was gone so we could play games or watch a movie on TV or something and he says Kyle, do you have any idea how much serious trouble your parents are in?

You probably noticed I haven't been writing much about them in here because what is the point? There is nothing I can do about them and things are going to happen the way they are going to happen. They have to let them out eventually, I said to Lorraine, because they didn't do anything. And Lorraine looks at me like he's just completely disgusted or like he's trying to decide if I'm his friend or not. Come on, he says, I have some people I want you to meet.

So we leave the house which right there is pretty serious because of the curfew which means kids are not supposed to be outside after 8 o'clock and we walk about ten blocks toward the river. There's a trail that goes along the water that the people who come off the boat like to walk on. We follow that for a while and then we step off the trail and go through some trees and follow the tracks for a bit until we come to a small part of town where there are all these trailers. I didn't even know there was a place with trailers in Cedar Falls. It's dark and I hear dogs barking but Lorraine says don't worry, I've been here a million times. I think I see about twenty trailers. When the dogs start barking I see some lights come on in some of the trailers, like people are wanting to see what the commotion is all about. We get to the end of one of the trailers and Lorraine tells me to wait there so I stand in the dark while he goes around and knocks on the door and then he's talking to someone but I can't hear what he's saying exactly. I just want him to finish what he's saying and come back for me because it's a little scary in the dark with all the dogs going, although the dogs by this time are starting to settle down a little.

Then Lorraine comes back for me. It's all clear, he says. I go with him to the door and we walk inside. I've never been in a trailer and it was very small inside. I had to duck my head so I didn't hit it on the door frame. There's a man and woman standing inside. They have white hair. Both of them. Not even gray. White. This is Betty and Frank, says Lorraine. Betty and Frank, I would like to present to you my friend Kyle. Betty says we are so glad to meet you, friend of Lorraine. And Frank says welcome my friend to our humble home. They talk kind of funny, but I like them right away. We have freshly baked cookies, says Betty, if you would like some. Lorraine doesn't say anything, so I don't say anything, only this isn't one of these times when I shouldn't say anything because Lorraine bumps me with his elbow a couple of times and says How about it, Kyle? Would you like some of Betty's homemade cookies? Then I say sure, I'd love some and she smiles real big and then I notice there is a kitchen behind her, a tiny little kitchen with a stove with only two burners and a fridge about half the size of a regular fridge and there is a plate of cookies on a tiny little counter next to the stove. Lorraine loves my cookies, says Betty, so I'm always sure to have some on hand. She puts the plate of cookies on this tiny table and we all four of us somehow sit around it.

Lorraine tells them what happened at school about the kid and the fight. Frank shakes his head. That's terrible, he says. Betty says yes it is terrible, but Kyle, don't you think you could have found a better way to handle the situation than attacking that boy? After all, he is obviously ignorant and bringing violence upon him will only reinforce his poor opinion of you by making him think you are not able to keep from letting your emotions cause physical damage to others. And right there I'm on the spot, because I know it was not such a good idea to hit the kid, but I couldn't help myself, only I don't know what to tell Betty. He was insulting my mom, I said, and then Betty's eyes got brighter in a funny way and she says I understand, Kyle. I do. But you know violent behavior rarely makes any situation better. Isn't that right, Frank? And Frank nods his head real slow. Now that's a fact I learned in the hills of Korea and I've never forgotten it. Lorraine tells me Frank was a soldier in the war in Korea, which I heard that happened about 65 years ago when the United States sent bombs and soldiers to this country called Korea, which is right next to China, which is who we are having a war with now.

My mom told me about that war, I say. How come so many people don't like war but they still happen? That's something we must all ask ourselves, says Betty. That's what your parents have done. Your mother and father are very brave people, said Frank. It is a crime that they are in jail. I eat some of my cookie, which is pretty good and I say I don't get what is right or wrong anymore. It's way too complicated. Then Betty laughs and Frank nods his head up and down real slow. You're right about that, Kyle, he says, you are absolutely right about that. Things can get very complicated indeed.

Then Lorraine tells me he needs to talk to Frank and Betty in private and he tells me to go look at the library and I think, what library? but then I see the other half of the trailer is all shelves on the walls and the shelves are stuffed with books, but not just books, also photocopies of books that are stapled together, just like the one Lorraine lent me about the mouse and then I figure out he must have gotten that book from Frank and Betty.

Feel free to borrow any book you want, says Betty, we try to have at least one copy of every book on the list. When she says the list she means the list of books we aren't supposed to read. Or even have. So Betty and Frank are a little bit like my parents. If they were caught with all these books then they would probably end up in jail just like my parents. I stand up from the table and walk back to the library while Lorraine leans close to Betty and Frank and they start whispering, which is a little bit weird with me standing there in the trailer but I think Lorraine is pretty smart so there must be a good reason for me being here so I just start looking at the books on the shelves. There are hundreds and hundreds. They are jammed into the shelves and books are stuffed on top of books so they are all squished together and in some places the books are two deep so you can't even see what the books are behind the books you can see. I never would have guessed this little trailer could hold so many books. I see books about how terrible war is. There is even a copy of the book my mother had me read that explained what war does to people. Also books I never heard of. Well, most of them I never heard of because they are on the list so you can't find them anywhere. Except they were all there in Betty and Frank's trailer.

A lot of the books are old and yellow, with the pages worn down. At first I'm afraid to even pick one up but then I see a pretty big one called A Light in the Attic which has some interesting drawings on the cover. I take it down and look at it. It is by a guy named Shel Silverstein. His picture on the cover shows him completely bald and he has a funny beard, plus he is barefoot and he's holding a guitar. The book is a bunch of poems with some wild characters and the words are different, not like what you hear people say usually. It's fun to read them because they make me laugh and the people in the poems spend a lot of their time being very different from what people are like in ordinary life. I keep reading the poems and I'm laughing. I can't help it. I just start laughing. Lorraine looks up from his conversation over at me. I'm sorry, I say, but this is a really funny book.

Betty and Frank let me borrow it. They said, be careful Kyle and I thought they meant I needed to take care of the book, but what they meant was I needed to be careful for myself, because I had the book and I could get into trouble by having it. So I haven't told anyone. I have the book here beside me right now. Not even Aunt Thelma knows I have it. She isn't awake yet from coming back late from her date with Les. I sure do write a lot more in this journal when I don't go to school, but I'm getting a little tired so I'll stop now. Oh yeah, did you notice the pen is different? I actually tried the pen Les gave me and it's not so bad. It writes pretty good.

March 2

Big news. My mom escaped. Yeah. Aunt Thelma told me. I don't know much else except I think she had help, because she was still at the hospital and outside the hospital, on the grass, there was an explosion and fire that some people had set so everyone in the hospital came out to see what was going on and even the guards who were supposed to be guarding my mom came out, and then she just walked out of the hospital. Yeah. I can hardly believe it. I asked my aunt where she is now but she doesn't know. So I'll have to find out later. She just got away. Some cops came to Aunt Thelma's house and asked us lots of questions about where she is. But we didn't tell them anything because we don't know anything. Then they went away. No way can my mother come here because then the police would know she was here and they would put her right back in jail. So in a way it is no different than when she was in jail because we still can't be in the same house or anything. So maybe it's not such big news after all. Plus my father is still in jail. You didn't forget about that, did you? Neither did I.

Remember I got that book from Betty and Frank's place? On the way back home that night Lorraine asks me why I got that book out of all the books that were there and I told him it looked fun. He said I know, but did it ever occur to you that Betty and Frank have a lot of the greatest books that have ever been written in that trailer and you took a silly book with silly poems in it? I told him the book was on the list so it had to be worth something because they only put good books on the list, right? He said not exactly, they mostly put books on the list they think are inappropriate. It doesn't mean they are great books or anything. I said what about Flowers for Algernon and he said that isn't a great book, Kyle, that's a good book, but not a great book. I'm talking about books like Beloved and 1984 and Brave New World and Left Hand of Darkness that are all about being different and surviving in conditions where survival is hard. It's about what it takes to survive and even maybe if it is worth surviving.

I asked him where the paintings were in Betty and Frank's trailer. He said what are you talking about. I said they had a little sign on one of the shelves that was like my mother's poster ART SAVES LIVES and then Lorraine tells me books are art too. It's not just pictures. Oh, I say. He tells me art is any type of creative expression, so books are art just as much as paintings are. I said does that mean when I write in my journal that's art too? He laughed. Sure, Kyle, that's art too. It's creative expression so it's art. Has to be, right? Now right there I don't know if he's kidding around or if he means it. I guess you can tell that about Lorraine sometimes. He says stuff where you don't know if he means what he says or if he's just being sarcastic.

After I talked to him I thought about it and I came to the conclusion that what my aunt Thelma wanted me to do is make this journal because it's art. She probably didn't tell me that because maybe she thought I wouldn't understand, but I do understand. It's like she said it would make all this about my parents easier if I could write it down in a book. So it's the same thing, it's ART SAVES LIVES. Only it's my life, even though I'm not the one put in jail or anything. And I'm going to be drafted, remember? In a few years I could maybe need my life to be saved just as much as anyone. Maybe more than everyone.

March 3

Oh man. I can hardly hold my pen to write this. My mom called. Yeah. We talked on the phone. Not for a long time because she said she had to be very careful. She had to throw the phone away as soon as she finished the call so no one could find her, but it was so great. She said not to worry about her. She was ok. I was going to tell her about the journal and everything, but she stopped me before I could say two words. You mustn't speak, she said. Let me do the talking. I'm taking a risk with this call and I won't let you say anything that could compromise us. I'm not going to see you for a long long time. But it doesn't mean I don't love you. Your father and I love you more than anything. I want you to listen to your aunt Thelma, Kyle, can you do that? Just answer yes or no. I said yes. I just wanted her to talk and talk for hours and hours but I knew that wasn't going to happen. She said we need you to be brave and believe in the future. Can you do that? she said. Can you do that Kyle? Just answer yes or no. I said yes. Then she said

I'm sorry if I sound mean but I have to be careful and you have to be careful too. You need to trust what happens next. Then she said bye. I wanted to tell her I was kicked out of school and Aunt Thelma had a boyfriend and I read Flowers for Algernon. I wanted to tell her everything, but I couldn't. If I did I would put her in danger. I'm not sure how, but maybe it would be like then the people who wanted to catch her would find out more about me and that would help them catch her or something. I don't know. I wanted to know where she was, but she could never tell me that, duh. So I just said bye. I miss you she said. And then it was over and I felt good and bad all at the same time, like it was nice to hear her but then it was not so nice that we couldn't say anything plus I didn't know where she was. Before she called I knew she was in a jail somewhere in Riverton and then she was in a hospital somewhere in Riverton. That was something. Now she could be anywhere and I could never know it.

So that's the big news of the day. I think I should be happy, but instead I just feel sad.

March 4

I forgot to say Lorraine is gone. I only wanted to write about my mother calling yesterday, but that wasn't the only thing that happened yesterday. Lorraine came over to my aunt Thelma's house. He had a backpack and mitts and a hat even though it wasn't that cold so I knew something was going on. He told me his parents were going to send him to a school where they try to brainwash you into being straight. I said is it like propaganda where they try to make you think a certain way and he said kind of, but not exactly. My parents say I'm gay and they want me to be ungay so they told me they're making me go to this school where I'll be drugged and have to submit to phony counseling and shit like that. It's also way religious, but I'm not going. No way. I'm getting out of Cedar Falls so this is good bye. I won't see you again. Oh, I said. I didn't know what else to say except I wondered if Betty and Frank had anything to do with this so I asked him and he said maybe you aren't so clueless after all, which sounds like it might be a nice thing to say but actually it was a little bit mean. That's how Lorraine is sometimes. He just has a different way, that's all. It's one of the things that makes him impressive.

I can't tell you a lot more details, he said, because you write everything down in that journal of yours and then I would be in jeopardy. I said, well of course I get it, my parents were arrested remember? He laughed and said, Right, I remember. So then he got all fancy talking. He said, It has been an honor knowing you, Kyle. I have valued our friendship and your at times naive insights. Which, again, sounds like a compliment or something, but is something else, if you know what I mean. But I always thought Lorraine was cool, so I said I hope everything is ok for you and he laughed and said, nothing is ok anymore, Kyle. The sooner you understand that, the better it will be for you. Perhaps we will meet again. If so, I look forward to it. Farewell. Then he was gone.

I remember in Flowers for Algernon how the guy was lonely at the end. That's how I'm feeling about now. More lonely than I've ever felt in my life.

March 5

I'm starting to wonder about how much I should be writing in this journal. This morning I almost tore it up into a million pieces because just by writing here I could be making it worse for people like Lorraine and my mom and dad if the police or other government people find it. And maybe Frank and Betty too. I was serious about it. I had the pages in my hand and I was going to tear them all out. I even started to rip it at the top but I stopped before I got too far. You can see how it's crinkled and torn in the corner. That's me almost destroying it. But I didn't. Why not? I don't know why not. The tear started going down the page and it was happening, the journal was getting ripped up, but then I couldn't go on. I just stopped. And when I stopped I felt better.

I thought about what Lorraine said, that writing is art. Maybe it's true and if the poster is right then I can't destroy something that saves lives, can I? That's just crazy. But what if I'm not saving lives is my question. What if I'm killing lives by writing here? I don't know which it is. But for now I'm keeping it. We'll see later if things get bad, which, according to Lorraine they already are and according to me, too, because everyone I know has to be super careful or else they will get into big trouble. It's crazy. Like today, Les came over for dinner that Aunt Thelma made for us. So it was all three of us at the dinner table eating and normally I would be embarrassed being around two grown-ups like that because they usually talk about stuff I don't know anything about. They have their own world is what I'm trying to say. And I think they must be embarrassed too, because they want to talk to you but they don't know what to say so they make up things to talk about that they wouldn't normally care about but they think you care about.

Like tonight Les starts asking me about skateboarding. He says, do you skateboard, Kyle? And I tell him no, I don't skateboard. And then he doesn't know what to say because he had already figured he was smart asking me about skateboarding because he thinks all boys my age skateboard. Well, a lot do but a lot don't. Then Aunt Thelma says you tried skateboarding once a couple of years ago Kyle, and I say I don't remember that and she says, sure Kyle, remember I got you a skateboard for your birthday because you wanted one. And I try to remember, and it comes back to me and I say, oh yeah, it was just one time and I never much liked it. Then Aunt Thelma smiles and Les smiles too because it's like he really did have something to ask me about that I had done when he asked me about skateboarding. So then he acted like we were best buddies and he says I don't blame you a bit, Kyle, I wouldn't get on a skateboard if you paid me. Ha ha. So then Aunt Thelma says, Kyle prefers going out into the woods, don't you Kyle. I say yes, but I don't say much more. Les says the woods are a good place to be. Aunt Thelma says, yes, that's true. And then Les just smiles at me. It was a little bit creepy if you want to know the truth.

OK, I think you get the picture about Les. And then he starts asking me about my mother. I heard your mother called, he said, that must have been nice. Just him asking made me feel sick, like my stomach was upset and I didn't want to answer him. I shrugged and nodded a little. I think it's terrible what's happening to her. I hope she's ok. Did she sound ok? I nodded. Could you tell where she was, Kyle? I bet you'd like to see her, wouldn't you? Did she say where she was? And now right there I was ready to just stop talking, even though

I hadn't said all that much up to then anyway. I mean, it was none of his business, right? Who did he think he was asking about my mother? That was personal stuff. The skateboarding was ok as far as being personal went, even though it was pretty lame of him, but my mother. Come on. And I notice Aunt Thelma is looking at him funny, so he must notice too because then he asks me if I have a girlfriend, like he's being so smart changing the subject and I tell him no and then he asks me if there are any pretty girls at school I like because he bets one of them would want me for a boyfriend and I'm thinking wait a minute, this guy is being weird and Aunt Thelma says there's plenty of time for girlfriends. Kyle is still a young man. And Les says, not that young since he is going to be defending our country in a couple of years, isn't that right, Kyle? You'll be handling a gun like a regular killer. And Aunt Thelma says we will have none of that talk at the table. Let's just be pleasant. Which finally stops Les. Which is ok with me. The point is Les is a pretty nosy guy and I'm not kidding. So how much should I write here? That's the question. What if Les finds my journal and reads it? I don't know, is what I'm saying. I just don't know.

March 6

What I tell myself over and over is my mom had a poster that said ART SAVES LIVES. So I want to believe it. But it's hard because of what I'm about to tell you in these next few pages, which might be the last things I'm ever going to write and you might not even get to read them at all because by this time tomorrow these pages could just be a pile of mush. But I need to explain what I'm talking about so here goes.

First of all Les came over for dinner tonight. We were all at the table again. Aunt Thelma went into the kitchen to get some stuff and Les says he's getting tired of all the vegetarian food around here. Aunt Thelma has started not eating dead animals either, just like me and my mom and dad. It wasn't anything I did, it was just what she decided. I tell Les I think vegetarian is ok. He laughs and then he tells me about Frank and Betty getting arrested. He didn't say Frank and Betty. He said isn't it a shame about that old couple in the trailer park getting arrested. And I said what old couple and he said didn't you hear about that Kyle? And then he looked at me like he wanted to reach into my brain or something. I know it sounds crazy but that's what it felt like and then Les said there is an old couple in town who give forbidden books to people. It's been going on for a while, but the police only found out about it today. All the books were impounded. They'll be evidence at their trial. Did you know them, Kyle?

All I could think about was I had that book with the funny poems. It was in my room. Plus I had this journal in my room where I tell where I got the book. So right there I knew I was about half an inch from getting into some major trouble and I just wanted Les to go away, but he wasn't going away. He was having dinner with us. It was like he and Aunt Thelma were practically married. So then he says it's even worse than the books, because according to the news reports, that old couple was part of a network that helps kids run away from their parents. Now isn't that a terrible thing, Kyle? Can you imagine people who would actually do that? Take kids away from their own family? Can you?

About this time Aunt Thelma came back from the kitchen and she says Les, why are you interrogating the boy? He doesn't know anything about that couple. And then Les gets this look on him like he's ready to break some bones and he says come on, Thelma. Open your eyes. And then everything gets still, like when they arrested my parents. Aunt Thelma looks at Les like he's some mess she has to clean up. It feels like the air is suddenly hard to breathe. Have you looked in his room, Thelma? Have you read his journal? Do you know anything about him? He was kicked out of school for a reason Thelma, and you're being purposely blind to it in the name of privacy. Don't you know privacy is dead? You need to find out why this boy is friends with a degenerate who has run away. You need to get to the core of his evil. And then Aunt Thelma's face falls. I don't know how else to describe. Her face slips down a tiny bit on her head, like she got super tired all of a sudden. Then she says you need to leave.

I think she means me and I feel scared all over again, like at the art gallery, scared like she's going to make me live on the sidewalk the way the soldiers in the book my mother gave me had to live and right there I start thinking about what I'm going to do. I would need to get away from Cedar Falls, I thought, just like Lorraine did, only he had help from Frank and Betty, and they're in jail now, so I would have to do it a different way, which feels even more scary because I don't know a different way, so it's going to be pretty hard. But then I see Aunt Thelma is actually talking to Les because he says Thelma, you don't want to kick me out of your house. But Aunt Thelma just says it again, she says You need to leave. You need to leave now. Les doesn't say anything and the whole house feels a little bit like when that guy at school called me and Lorraine names, like something bad was going to happen. Les looks at me. The police are going to come around, you know. They'll figure out you were friends with that kid and they're going to want to ask you questions. Now! said Aunt Thelma real loud. I want you gone NOW. So finally Les stands up and gets his dorky security guard jacket and leaves.

Then Aunt Thelma falls into a chair and she's shaking like she's so scared she can't even say anything. I feel bad for her, but I'm also scared the police will come in and find that book and my journal. I'm sorry Kyle, says Aunt Thelma. I'm so sorry I ever met him and went out with him. I'm sorry I invited him into my house and I'm sorry I exposed him to you. I never should have done that, Kyle. Never. I said it's ok, it's ok. He didn't hurt me or anything. He was just a dumb old jerky guy is all. There's plenty of those around. Aunt Thelma laughs and I laugh too. Then she asks me if I knew that couple Les was talking about. I probably shouldn't have said anything, but I already wrote it here, so it's not like I've kept it a total secret, so I said I did.

She said I don't think there's anything wrong with reading any of those books, Kyle, but life is different now. What I think and what the authorities think are two different things, and they are the ones with the power. Do you understand? I say yeah. Aunt Thelma says if you get caught with any of them, they could kick you out of school. Then she blinks, and her eyes go funny and then she says Oh yeah. Too late. I tell her I have one of the books. She says let me see it. I go and get the book with the poems and show it to her. She looks about as surprised as anyone can be. You got this from that couple? I tell her yes. Why would something like this be forbidden? She shakes her head. It's a crazy world, Kyle, we are living in a crazy world. I don't say anything. Do you have any other books from them? I tell her no. She takes a deep breath. That's good. It makes our job easier.

Then she gets two scissors from out of the drawer. She hands one to me. I'm sorry to have to do this, she says, but we need to protect ourselves. We can't have this in the house. She rips out some pages and hands them to me. Thin strips, she says. She rips out some more pages and starts cutting them up with the scissors. Pretty soon she has a pile of paper strips on the table. I know I'm supposed to do the same thing, but I can't make myself. The book has pictures inside it. It feels wrong to cut up other people's pictures. I don't want to do it. Aunt Thelma looks at me. This isn't something I want, she says. They're making us. We have to destroy this book. It's for our own good. I have the scissors in my hand.

I remember my mom said once that people need art. They need it just as much as they need food. I thought it was a crazy thing to say but I thought about it again while I watched Aunt Thelma rip out those pages and cut them into tiny pieces. My mother is about the smartest person I know, so if she says something then you have to think about it. That's why I wasn't helping Aunt Thelma. Because that book with the poems and the drawings, it was art, just like Lorraine said. You shouldn't wreck art. You just shouldn't. It was wrong. Aunt Thelma gave me the paper cover that wraps around the book. I cut out the picture of Shel Silverstein. Can I keep this part? I said to Aunt Thelma. She looked at the picture. I don't know, Kyle. If they found it, they could maybe tell it came from a forbidden book. We could put it in one of the photo albums I said. He could be one of our relatives who lives far away and dresses different from us. Aunt Thelma picked up the picture and looked at the man who wrote the poems we were cutting up into tiny strips of paper. I just don't know if it's safe, she says. Please please please, I say, and I don't even know why I want to save his picture, but I want to have something from this book. We can't just completely destroy it because Betty and Frank wouldn't want that, and Lorraine wouldn't want that, even if he didn't think it was the best one for me to get, and my mother and father wouldn't want that either.

So finally Aunt Thelma says ok Kyle, if that's what you want you can keep the picture but you don't have to put it in the album. I tell her thanks and then I start cutting up the book with her. It is real quiet in the house. Aunt Thelma doesn't say anything, and I don't want to say anything either. She gets up and goes into the living room and turns on the TV so the sound fills up the house. After she did that, things felt better. We kept cutting up the pages.

When all the pages were in tiny pieces in a pile on the table, she took the covers and tried cutting them up, only it didn't work because the scissors were too small. So she bent the boards with her hands. It's hard to do because they are so thick, but she worked at it and finally they started bending and breaking. I helped her. While I'm breaking up the cover she went to a cabinet and pulled down a blender. She took some of the paper strips and put them in the blender with some water and then started up the blender on the highest speed. In no time at all the strips of paper and water turned into a gray mush. She dumped the mush into the sink and turned on the trash disposer. There, she said. There's no way they can trace that back to us and even if they did, there's no way to tell what it was. We did the same thing to the rest of the paper and then to the covers. Aunt Thelma stood over the sink as the last of the mush got washed down. This is just about the saddest day of my life, she says.

Then she said, Kyle, I hate to ask this of you, because I gave that journal to you and I know you've been diligent about writing in it, but it is a dangerous book now. It must have all kinds of things in it that could get us into serious trouble. She didn't have to say anything else. I knew what she meant. She meant we were going to have to turn my journal into mush, just like the book of poems. I said no Aunt Thelma no. You can't make me do that. Can't we hide it somewhere? I want my mother to read it when she finds me. Please Aunt Thelma.

Please. And she says it isn't something I want to do, just like I didn't want to destroy the poetry book, but you must see how important it is, Kyle. Then all of a sudden I was mad at everyone because Aunt Thelma wanted me to write this journal and now she was saying no Kyle, we have to turn it to mush. And it's not just that it's mine. There's more than that. Because I've been talking to my mother and father all this time. That's what the journal is and I don't want to let it get put through the blender because there's only one. I say, but my journal isn't on that list. They can't say we are doing something wrong because it's not on the list. It's not. Aunt Thelma shakes her head. She says that doesn't matter. Did you write about Betty and Frank? Did you write about your friend Lorraine? And I say yeah, I did. And then she says, that's the problem, Kyle. They can find it and take it and use it as evidence against us. Both of us. I have to protect you. I promised Allie.

I started thinking about how to save the journal. I said, can't we put it somewhere they can't find it? Where? said Aunt Thelma. We could bury it, I said. Aunt Thelma said, I don't think so. I said, can't we wait just a little bit? She said ok, Kyle. We can wait till the morning. Maybe something will come to us. You understand I don't want to do this, don't you

Kyle? You see we are being forced into this? You understand what's going on, don't you? I kind of do but I kind of don't. I know my parents should never have been put in jail and now I'm starting to think that just because it's a big mistake does not mean someone is going to fix the big mistake. So we have to fix it. Us. Our family. And Aunt Thelma is just trying to make it so we have a better chance of being a family again. I know that's what she's doing, but it's still hard. She said write a last entry in the journal, Kyle. Write it tonight and tomorrow we'll figure out what to do with the journal. So that's what I'm doing. That's all I've been doing for the last three hours because once I remember my father saying art is not just the paint on a canvas, art is something spiritual. Once it is created, it lives beyond the physical world. I hope that's true. I hope this journal is more than just a bunch of paper that can turn into mush.

I'm starting to think this journal is like my shadow person. It's not me, not really, but in a way it is me, because I wrote it and maybe you're reading it two hundred years from now and I'm gone, but I'm not gone. I'm right here in this journal. It's me. I don't want to turn to mush.

Book 2

March 9

First of all, I'm not back in school even though my six days are up. Second of all, this is a new journal, which I guess I don't have to tell you because you can see that just by looking at it, and it's not like my other journal because it's a book where captains of boats write what happens on their boat. That's why the lines are different. It's called a ship's log, even though this isn't a ship's log, it's just me and my journal, but it's what was here. Malcolm gave it to me. I'll tell you about him later. And third of all, I'm not at my aunt Thelma's anymore. I'm on a sailboat.

So maybe you think me and my aunt Thelma turned my first journal to mush. Wrong. She woke me up in the middle of the night after I had written that long part about the dinner with Les and how we turned the poem book to mush. After that I glued in Shel Silverstein's picture at the end of the journal. Funny bald guy. I just liked his picture because he looked like this kind of person you don't see much. At least not me. So if you are a future historian, then maybe you have only this book which means you don't have an important part of my life, but I'm not going to repeat it all here for you. That would be impossible for one thing because that first book took me a lot of weeks to write and I don't have weeks to write it all over again, plus I wouldn't be able to remember all the things I put in there. So I guess you'll have to go find that other journal. Good Luck.

In the meantime I'll tell you about what happened in the morning 3 days ago. My aunt Thelma wakes me up. We'll mail your journal to your grandfather, she says. I say, will that work? She shrugs. It's our best try. I think, well, I won't have it anymore, but at least it'll be alive. And then I laugh at myself, thinking of the journal as if it could be alive or dead. But when you see a book turn into a pile of gray mush like Shel Silverstein's book, then you know what dead is. So I tell my aunt Thelma, that is a good idea. And she smiles and laughs a little herself. I'm glad you think so, Kyle. I think it'll work. I wrote a note to your grandfather so he'll know what it is when he gets it. She says should I tell him not to read it? I try to remember if there is anything in it that would be embarrassing to me or if I said anything about my grandfather that he wouldn't like to read but I don't remember anything like that in the journal, so I say it's ok if he reads it. Aunt Thelma says are you sure and I say yeah I'm sure and she says fine.

So she finds a cardboard box and we put the journal into the box and then we put in her little note and then we find some newspapers and bunch them up and stuff them into the box to protect the journal. We closed up the box and taped it. Then Aunt Thelma got some stamps and stuck them on the box. There were pictures of President Cooper on the stamps, only she wasn't torturing anyone. Ha ha. Lame joke. Never mind. It was actually a picture of President Cooper looking up at the sky where there are a row of flags waving. Her eyes were so bright on the stamp, like they weren't real eyes. I was going to ask my aunt Thelma if that was art too, but then I decided I didn't have to. Of course the pictures on the stamps are art. It's a picture someone made. It doesn't matter if you didn't like the person in the picture or if you thought they were wrong about things or even if you didn't vote for them. It was still a picture of a person. It was still art. And it was going to make sure my journal got to my grandfather, so even if it didn't save lives, it was going to save my journal, which I already said earlier that it is almost the same as saving lives because the journal is an alive thing in a way. It was funny seeing so many pictures of President Cooper on the box. All those flags. She paid more attention to flags than to people like my mother and father who no way should be in jail or running away from jail. But I won't go into that now. Except I'll say it again here because if you didn't read the first journal then you didn't see this: MY PARENTS ARE NOT TERRORISTS.

So the package was all ready, except for the address. Aunt Thelma looked in the kitchen drawer and found an address book. It's been a while since I mailed anything to my father, she said as she riffled through the addresses. Here it is. She wrote the address on the outside of the box. It's too much postage, she said, but it's better to have it go over than have it not be enough because then the post office would just send it back to us. Are you ok with this? she said. I nodded. All right then, she said. Let's take this down to the post office. I said, You mean now? What about curfew? She said it's 8 in the morning. Curfew is over.

So we put on our jackets and mitts and went outside. It was pretty cold. The post office is only about five blocks away. We got to it and went inside. There was a small line. I looked around and saw posters on the wall. One of them had President

Cooper pointing her finger at us. The words underneath said: SAVE A LIFE: REGISTER FOR THE DRAFT. Another one had a picture of a soldier with a gun and a bayonet. On the bayonet there were little Chinese guys stuck through like chunks of meat on a shish kebob. The words at the bottom said: BUY WAR BONDS: HELP ME STICK IT TO THE YELLOWS. I thought: That's what they want me to do. I didn't like that. When we got to the front of the line the guy made us open the package. We have to see everything that goes out of this office, he said. So Aunt Thelma untaped the box and showed the guy my journal. I was so nervous he was going to take it but he didn't. He flipped through it. This some kind of homework or something? he said. It's a family history, said Aunt Thelma. My nephew here wants to give it to my father. The clerk stops at the picture of Shel Silverstein, and looks at it closely. That's my brother Max, says Aunt Thelma. He's the family eccentric. The guy laughs and retapes the package with my diary inside. Then we leave. So that's that, said Aunt Thelma. Yeah, I say. That's that. So now you know why I started this second journal. But you still don't know why I'm on a boat. That's complicated and I can't tell you all at once. So I'll do it a little bit at a time.

After we mailed my journal we went back to Aunt Thelma's house. I was going to just go back to sleep, but Aunt Thelma said wait Kyle. I have a meeting with the lawyer today and when she told me that I thought maybe some good news was about to happen, but she said, don't get too excited. It's just a progress report and I don't think he has a lot to tell me, but I also think he wants more money so we have to have a meeting. And I said, why does he want more money when he hasn't done anything? And also, now only Dad is in jail, so the lawyer bills should be only half what they were before and Aunt Thelma says, that makes sense in a funny way, but that's not the way things are done. Of course not, I think, because that would make sense and I figured out a long long time ago that a lot of things make absolutely no sense at all.

Aunt Thelma says why don't you come with me to the lawyer's? It's about your parents, after all. So I say ok. We have breakfast and then we get in Aunt Thelma's car and drive to the lawyer's office. It was about 10 o'clock by this time. But I am close to finishing writing here for today because I'm feeling pretty tired right now. I still haven't told you about the boat. The boat is my escape vessel. That's what Malcolm calls it and I guess he should know since it's his boat. Also I don't know where Aunt Thelma is. But don't get mad at me. It's not my fault we split up. Anyway, she might be back home now, but I doubt it. I think she's on some kind of escape route herself. She could be on a boat too. Or on some kind of other escape vehicle, like a car maybe. Or she could be anywhere, just like my mother. Anyway she's not with me. I'm on my way to Canada. I need to sleep now. I'll write more here tomorrow.

March 10

Malcolm says all great water journeys have been recorded in diaries. I say ok. He's talking about ship's logs which is where the captain of the ship writes down where they are exactly and what supplies and people are on the ship, and what happens to them as they go along. For example, if people on the boat get married the captain would put that in the log or if some passenger stole something from another passenger then the captain would put that in the log, or if a passenger got sick. Obviously, that isn't going to happen on this boat where I am now because there's only me and Malcolm and it's a small boat, but he was just saying that boats and journals go together. So I guess I'm writing a ship's log, even though I'm not the captain or anything. Malcolm is the captain because it's his boat. It's a sailboat with a small part called the cabin where we can get in out of the rain and cold. That's where I am right now. It's in the middle of the day. Malcolm is outside making sure the sails are working right. He's on the deck. I've been on the deck with him a couple of times. It's fun to watch the shore pass by, but he doesn't let me stay up there long. We still have to keep you a secret, he says, until we get to Canada, so you need to stay below decks. That's what he told me the first day. I asked him if he had some paper for me to write on. He found a blank ship's log and gave it to me. I told him I like to write a diary. And let me tell you I never in my life thought I would ever say anything like that. But it's true. So I took the log and said thank you a lot and started writing in it.

Malcolm told me the path we're supposed to take. Only he said I should call it a route. That's what sailors say. Our route is going to follow the river to the ocean, then head north along the coast until we get to Vancouver Island. Malcolm said he didn't know what would happen next, but he guessed there will be other people who will get me and take me to somewhere safe. He asked me if I had any family in Canada. I told him about my grandfather. He said, then I'll bet that's what they have planned, they'll take you to him. And the beauty part of all this is I don't have to do any homework because I don't have to go to school. Ha ha.

But I think I'm probably getting you all confused with the story. So I better go back to the lawyer meeting. Aunt Thelma said I should come to the meeting with her because the lawyer needs to understand there is a child involved who has been without his parents for over a month now and SOMETHING has to be done. The lawyer's office is in Riverton, so we drive there for half an hour. I ask Aunt Thelma if the lawyer is worth the money she's giving him but she doesn't say much except that she is starting to wonder about that herself. Amen to that, I say. And she laughs, like I told a joke even though I wasn't trying to.

We get to Riverton a little early for the appointment, so we go to a coffee shop. Aunt Thelma gets a coffee for herself and a donut for me and we sit at a table near the window. I watch the people go by and the light rail train stop and let off more people. The coffee shop is real busy. Some woman is walking from the counter with her coffee and she bumps into Aunt Thelma's chair. She says excuse me, I'm sorry, I am such a klutz, and then she drops a little slip of folded up paper into Aunt Thelma's lap, and then the woman is gone so fast I wondered if she had really even been there. Aunt Thelma didn't even notice there was a piece of paper on her lap. So I lean close to her and whisper: Aunt Thelma, that person dropped something. She looks down and blinks and says It has my name on it. So right there I knew it wasn't some accident. That woman wanted Aunt Thelma to have the paper. Aunt Thelma picks it up and her face turns white. I see the paper has the word Cat on it. It's Allie's handwriting, whispers Aunt Thelma. At first I think she's joking, but she's not. She looks around the coffee shop for a second. No one is looking at her or me. What does it say? I whisper. She unfolds the paper and reads it. What does she say? I ask again. Three times. Then she gives it to me to read. Here's what it said, more or less the way I remember it.

Dear Cat and Kyle. Forget the lawyer. Buy tickets on the sternwheeler for today and get on board. Prepare for a long journey. Trust what happens next. Destroy this note. I love you both, Allie.

When I saw those words, trust what happens next, I knew the note was from my mother. The next thing I know we're back in the car and we're driving pretty fast to get back to Cedar Falls because Aunt Thelma says the sternwheeler leaves town a little before 4 o'clock so we have to make sure we're going to be on it. I say will my mother be on the sternwheeler? Is that why she wrote that note? But Aunt Thelma says I don't know Kyle. I say I hope she is because she escaped from the hospital and she wouldn't just run away forever so we never see her or anything. She wants to get back to us, only she can't just come back to town, right, because then the police would find her again, so she is going to be on the sternwheeler. Isn't that right? I say. Isn't that right Aunt Thelma? Aunt Thelma, isn't that right?

I know I'm repeating myself but I'm trying to be accurate here because I really *did* repeat myself over and over. It was because I was all excited that I might see my mother again so don't think I was crazy or anything. But Aunt Thelma doesn't say a thing to me except she said when they were younger, not when they were kids, but when they were grown up, only not all the way grown up, that my mother talked about what they would do if the world ever became dangerous. Aunt Thelma said my mother would find a way to make sure we would at least be a family and be together. She always said that, Kyle. It was very important to her. So I said, then she will be on the boat. She will.

Only Aunt Thelma still didn't agree with me. She said we just need to be on that sternwheeler, Kyle. I don't know what will happen next. I just don't know, but if it's what Allie wants, then we should do it. I know that much. So we get back home and put some clothes into small backpacks and Aunt Thelma locks up the house and we go down to the port. We buy tickets for the sternwheeler which is floating at the end of the dock. Funny thing is I have lived in Cedar Falls all my life and the sternwheeler stops here just about every week but I've never been on it so I'm excited even if my mother doesn't turn out to be there, which I was so sure she was going to be that I could hardly even wait for Aunt Thelma to get the tickets. But there's a line so we have to wait and then she finally gets the tickets and we walk out to the dock and guess who's there at the bottom of the ramp. It's Les. He's standing against the rail, leaning back all casual like and looking like he is waiting for us or something.

So right away I get a little nervous, because how could he even know we were going to get a ticket for the sternwheeler? Aunt Thelma slows down her walk when she sees him. She doesn't say anything, but she grabs my hand and then she starts walking faster and I have to run a little to keep up and we walk past Les, who just stares at us and smiles, but it's not a smile that makes you feel good, it's more a smile that's not a smile. We go to the end of the ramp and then we're inside the sternwheeler and we walk through these narrow halls and take a few turns and go up some stairs and end up on the top of the sternwheeler. The top deck.

Aunt Thelma says, What is Les doing here? I don't answer because for one thing how would I know? and for another thing, she's asking the air, not me. Can I look for my mother? I say. No, Kyle, she says. I want you close to me. Then you come with me to look for her, I say. But Aunt Thelma says no, Kyle. She is watching Les, who is still on the dock. I pull on Aunt Thelma's hand. She turns around and grabs me by the shoulders. Your mother is not on board, Kyle, she says. I say, How do you know. She says, she just isn't. Get that through your head, and as she's saying this she's shaking me, which is something she has never done before, so it's pretty serious. She doesn't shake me for a long time. I don't get hurt or anything. She was just upset about Les. But I pull back from her anyway, and I run away. She calls my name but I don't answer.

I run to the stairs and go down them and run down a hallway. There are lots of doors in the hallway which open up to cabins where people stay while they are on the sternwheeler. So my mom could be in one of these rooms. I hear Aunt Thelma coming down the stairs behind me. Kyle, she shouts. Kyle! Come back. But I just keep running. I get to the end of the hall, and it curves around and there are more stairs. I go down them and there are more halls. I run and pretty soon I'm basically completely lost. But there are people walking everywhere. They completely ignore me as I run by them. I look at all of them because one of them could be my mother. But you know by now my mother wasn't any of them. I'm just telling you what I was hoping for. I didn't see my mother. But I saw Les walking down the hall. I didn't like seeing him. It wasn't just how he thought there was something wrong with me, I also didn't like him because he made my aunt Thelma nervous, and I also didn't like him because he was just creepy. Let's just say he had a lot of things about him I didn't like. So when I saw him I made sure he didn't see me. I ducked around some people, and doubled back the way I came, then went up top again. Aunt Thelma wasn't there anymore. I had my ticket in my pocket, with my room number on it. Only I didn't have a key, so I could go to the room, but then I would only be standing outside it, unless Aunt Thelma was there, so I decided I wouldn't go to my room yet.

Instead I ran to the other end of the boat, what Malcolm would say is called the stern, and I found a place where the stairs go around a pole and then there's this place where I can get behind the stairs and under them, so I did that. It was a little bit dark in there and I could hear people's feet going up and down the stairs right over my head and the stairs shook and clanged as they walked. But no one saw me. I was safe from Les and Aunt Thelma. Not that I was scared of Aunt Thelma, that's not what I'm saying, even though she shook me and everything because you have to understand she isn't like that normally. She's under a ton of stress because of my parents and having me in the house and everything. Remember, she doesn't even like to have cats in her house, which is funny because her nickname is Cat. But anyway, all I'm saying is I just needed some time to think.

So pretty soon the sternwheeler starts moving real slow. It rocks a little, and my head and stomach feel a little bit weird. There was also the sound of the wheel turning around, which was going on behind the ship because it's a sternwheeler, get it? I looked through the stairs and I saw a lot of people walking around. They were all relaxed and not scared a bit. Which, I know, why should they be? Right, but the thing is I'm pretty scared about a lot of things so it seems weird when no one else is. But that's the way it is. You can be one thing and everyone else can be another thing and it doesn't mean anything because everyone is different.

     Mario Milosevic

I think I should get out from under the stairs, but after a while I like it there. I think I could stay there forever. I see Aunt Thelma come down the hall a couple of times. She looks so upset. You don't have to be a genius to know she's looking for me. I think maybe I should come out and let her see me, but I don't. I know it's mean, but I guess I was still mad a little bit. Maybe even a lot. So I just wait. I wait until it is dark. The hall lights go dim. Not off, just not as bright. There are almost no people in the hall. Then I come out.

Malcolm says I sure fill up the pages in this log book. I tell him what else do I have to do if you won't let me be topside? He laughs and says, you have a point. What did you do in your town? Skateboard a lot?

Yeah. Skateboarding. I think grown-ups must think every kid ever born just lives to skateboard and drools whenever they see a skateboard or even thinks about a skateboard or hears the word skateboard. Only when Malcolm asked it wasn't like when Les asked. Malcolm is way cooler than Les. I'm pretty sure Les could never be a sailboat pilot, for one thing. So I tell Malcolm no I don't skateboard, and he says, Ah, then, you must be a lady's man and I say what do you mean and he says I bet all the girls in school want you for a boyfriend. So I say I guess you would have to ask them about that, but I kind of doubt it. And then he laughs, like I told a joke. I think I'm supposed to laugh too, only I don't see the joke, so I just smile and I tell him about some of the places I like to hike, like this one trail that goes for about two miles through the woods and you follow this creek the whole way. There are old growth trees about three hundred years old there and at the end of the trail there's this 500 foot tall waterfall. It's got three sections: the top part is like a giant wedding cake where the water flows over it all white like icing, the middle part is a flatter section that goes fast like rapids, and the third part, on the bottom, is where the water free falls over a cliff into a pool at the bottom. When it's cold, the mist all freezes around it into these huge ice slabs. It's pretty amazing and I tell Malcolm that I really like going there. He says that is fantastic, Kyle. It sounds like a marvelous place. I would love to visit it some day, maybe when things are different in the United States. I tell him about the mushrooms that grow in the fall and the flowers that grow in the spring. Pretty soon I think I'm boring him to death but he listens to every word and he looks like he's interested so it was fun telling him.

Then he gets serious and says it should only be another day or two before we get to Vancouver Island. From there, he says, you'll be out of my hands and in the care of another. I don't know where you'll go next, but we've been doing this sort of thing for a while, and we take care of the people we rescue. I ask him who we is. We're patriots, says Malcolm. We're people who believe in freedom and we don't think anyone should be persecuted for their opinions or their expression of those opinions. You mean like my mother and father? I say. Exactly, says Malcolm, like your mother and father. Do you know where my mother is? I say. He tells me no. To maintain safety, we work by knowing as few people as possible, he says. It's an exercise in faith and belief.

He tells me about this thing called the underground railroad which happened a long time ago and it was when slaves were helped to get away from places where they were slaves and what he is doing with me is the same thing. It wasn't a real railroad. It was just people who were slaves walking, but they called it a railroad because there were these stations where they stopped along the way where they could get food and some sleep and be hidden, so the stations were like railroad stations.

But I'm not a slave, I said, and Malcolm said No, you aren't, but some of your freedoms have been taken from you. It's a very similar thing. He says, don't worry is all I'm saying to you Kyle. There are people who will get you to where you need to be. Trust what happens next. Then he went back topside to make sure we weren't sailing into a rock or anything. (We weren't.)

So now I'll tell you more about the sternwheeler. Once it was dark, I figured it was safe to get out from under the stairs and search for my mother. Now, look, I know I must sound stupid to keep looking for her when Aunt Thelma said about a million times she wasn't there, but I had to find out for myself, ok?

So I go back to that first hallway, where all the doors were and I knock on the first cabin. A man opens the door and looks at me. Yeah? he says. I'm looking for my mother. Her name is Alice. You got the wrong cabin, kid, he says and slams the door shut. I think, ok. First door down. I'll go to the next one. I knock. A woman opens the door. She doesn't even let me say anything. Are you the young man they're all looking for? she says. I don't say a word. I just run. I run down the hall and go up the stairs to the next deck and I find the door that is my cabin and try pushing it open but it is locked, so I knock on the door and Aunt Thelma opens it. Her face is so red and her eyes are all puffy and I feel bad right away because I'm pretty sure it's all about me, and she grabs my arm and pulls me inside and then slams the door shut and I'm about ready to get the snot beat out of me so I'm getting myself prepared for it, but instead she just hugs me about as hard as she can. And she says she's sorry for shaking me.

Then she stops hugging me and asks me where I've been. I tell her I needed time to think so I hid out under some stairs. Did you see Les? she said. I told her I did but he didn't see me. Then I ask her why Les is so interested in us. She says she doesn't know except she's pretty sure he's trying to get information about my parents. But we don't know anything about where they are, I said. I know that, Kyle, but he thinks he can find out something from us. He's actually a dumb guy, to tell you the truth. I'm sorry I ever went out with him.

I looked around the cabin, which was so small, and there were two tiny beds and a window between them and in one corner a tiny desk with a chair. I saw a picture on the desk. It was a drawing of me. What is this? I said. Aunt Thelma said I found some paper and a pen in the drawer, so I started drawing. I haven't drawn in years, but I was so scared something awful happened to you, that I had to do something to keep from going crazy. What do you think of it? I picked up the drawing. It looked exactly like me so I knew Aunt Thelma was a real artist. I told her it was a nice picture and she seemed to like that. She smiled and her eyes got bright. Is this what that poster my mother had means? Did drawing this picture save Aunt Thelma's life?

So then I think it must be time for us to get some sleep, even though I'm not all that tired. The boat is slowing down. We both notice it. I guess we're going to be docking, says Aunt Thelma. I figure we must be at Salmon Rapids. That's the next town on the river after Cedar Falls and it has a big Casino that's open 24 hours a day. Before I say anything, there's a small knock at the door. Aunt Thelma's eyes go super wide. She puts a finger to her lips. I keep quiet. Who is it? says Aunt Thelma. I'm here to help you, says a woman's voice. Trust what happens next and let me in. Aunt Thelma looks at me. Should I? she says. Ask them if they know where my mother is, I whisper. She nods. We can get you to your family, says the voice. Aunt Thelma opens the door. A woman comes in. Hi, she says. She is wearing a purple jacket. It's good you followed the directions on the note. We have a small craft waiting. Come with me. I stuff Aunt Thelma's drawing of me into my backpack. Aunt Thelma grabs her purse, and we follow the woman down the hall to the boarding ramp. Lots of other people are in the hall too, going in the same direction. We see

Les. He is standing near the exit, the big dork. He waves at us and smiles his creepy smile. I don't wave back. Good luck on the slots, he says. Aunt Thelma pulls me closer to her. We follow the woman with the purple jacket down the ramp and we are in downtown Salmon Rapids. A ton of people from the sternwheeler keep walking to the casino. We follow the crowd for a while and then the woman in purple steers us down a path back toward the river, but away from the sternwheeler. We have to be careful where we step because it's hard to see in the dark. We end up at a little bay, where there is a small motor boat. We all three get into the boat and the woman in the purple jacket starts up the motor. She steers the little boat away from the shore into the river. The motor is making too big a noise for us to say anything, but it isn't so big that it is louder than the waves. The woman in purple revs the motor so we're hitting the waves hard and the boat rocks up and down. I hear Aunt Thelma shout as loud as she can: Where are we going? The woman doesn't turn around, but she shouts so we can hear. To a safe place, she says. Trust what happens next.

I start to notice it's getting pretty cold out and we don't exactly have real warm clothes. There are life jackets in the bottom of the boat. I pick them up and give one to Aunt

Thelma. She takes it and puts it on. I put on the other one. It doesn't keep me warm, but it still feels good to have it on.

I look behind me and the sternwheeler is getting smaller. We're going in the same direction it was going, following the river, but we're going much faster than it went and it's a lot darker because this little boat has no lights at all. The water is black around us. I can't see the shore. It feels like we're on the ocean. We go for about half an hour I think. It's hard to be sure. I see some lights on the shore that are supposed to help guide boats away from the shore because the river doesn't just go straight, it has a lot of turns. We pass a couple of giant barges filled with wood chips and another one with big loads of wheat. I've seen them on the river before but they look so much bigger when you are right next to them. They look like they could roll right over us and we'd be gone in a second and they wouldn't even notice we were ever there. Then we steer over to the bank where there's a little inlet disguised by some trees, which I can just barely make out in the dark. The pilot starts slowing way down just as the boat makes this scraping sound where it's touching the sand. OK, she says, everybody out. Aunt Thelma grabs my arm and we step off the boat into a few inches of water, so our feet get wet. We wade to the shore which is sandy and has shells all over it. I think the pilot is going to step off too, but no. She says good luck and then she pushes the boat back into the river, revs up the engine and she's gone.

Aunt Thelma says What the F, and she doesn't even apologize for cursing in front of me. So now we're stuck on the river bank with no food or water or anything, plus it's pretty cold. I can hear the cars on the expressway a little way off, but there is a pretty thick bunch of trees in the way, and anyhow, we can't just walk up to the expressway and get someone to drive us somewhere. What I'm trying to say here is we were marooned and we had no idea what we were going to do next.

March 12

Malcolm says this is my last day on his sailboat which he calls The Sharon. That's the way he says it. Not plain Sharon, but *The* Sharon. That's how sailors say it when they want to talk about their ship. I ask him who Sharon is. He tells me Sharon is the name of his girlfriend, who lives in Vancouver BC with him. I said, does Sharon ever come on the sailboat with you? He said we sail together all the time. We really enjoy it, but she didn't want to come on this trip. The cabin can get pretty crowded with three people. I asked where he learned to drive a sailboat. He said he learned to *pilot* a sailboat from his parents while growing up in Riverton and spending a lot of time on the water. Right there, in case you didn't notice, I used the wrong word. It's pilot, not drive. But he didn't make me feel stupid by telling me I was wrong. He just used the right word and let me figure it out on my own, which is pretty cool in a way, even if in another way he was making me talk the way he wanted me to talk. Someone might think that's like propaganda, but it isn't. Not really. I think I already told you I like Malcolm a lot. I said, did his parents still live there and he said yes and he missed them a lot but he moved away from the United States when he started seeing how the country was going with the crack down on freedoms and expression. Now Malcolm and Sharon help other people to get out of the country, like me. I said I didn't know that is what I was doing. He looked surprised when I said that. Kyle, he said, you must know your mother can never go back to your town or be in the country anymore, at least officially. I asked him if he knew where my mother was. He said he didn't know, but there are people in the network who are taking care of her. The thing is, he said, it's more difficult with your mother because she is much more high profile and needs to be way more careful so her case is more complicated than yours.

I told him I understood, even though I'm not sure I did. Good, he said, then he cooked us a big lunch. He has a little kitchen in the sailboat, even smaller than the one in Frank and Betty's trailer. I asked him if he knows Frank and Betty. He said no. Are they friends of yours? I said Yeah, even though I only ever met them once, but they had all these books in their trailer and they lent me one. Me and my aunt Thelma ended up putting it through a blender so we could be safe. Malcolm nodded when I told him that, like he knew exactly what a sad thing it was we did.

Malcolm made toast and scrambled eggs and sausages on the stove while I told him about Frank and Betty and how they ended up in jail. Malcolm said there are a lot of brave people trying to do what they can, but sometimes that isn't enough. Sometimes you have to run. He said it like it was about the most serious thing anyone had ever said in their entire lives. The last straw for us, for Sharon and me, was when Cooper pushed through those amendments to the constitution that said foreign combatants were to be considered sub human and not subject to any kind of humanitarian consideration. That was a sad sad day, Kyle. It made the war with China inevitable, and the things that have been done to Chinese prisoners of war are too horrible for any country to do to them, much less this country. My former country.

I told Malcolm I didn't know about any of that because there were people who thought we were doing the right thing by fighting China because they were trying to steal oil from other countries and anyway the Chinese probably do bad things to our POWs. Malcolm said that was true, but right and wrong is right and wrong. We shouldn't be torturing anyone. I said some of the soldiers who went wanted to go. They decided completely on their own. There were lots who weren't even drafted, so they must think it is an important thing to do. Malcolm said you have been thinking about this, haven't you? I said, well sure, it's pretty important. Yes, said Malcolm, it is important. And most people do things they think are right, and sometimes we won't know if they were right or wrong until a long time has passed, until historians look at the evidence and make judgments. But people who are living history don't have that luxury. We have to make decisions on what we think is right as it happens, and too much of what my former country has been doing is just plain wrong. They torture POWs, but it's all completely legal because by law the Chinese are now considered to be less human than Americans. Do you understand, Kyle? Do you see how wrong that is? We should not be doing such things.

I said I know people do wrong things. It was wrong of them to put my parents in jail. Malcolm said that's a perfect example. Then I said, but what if the Chinese guys have information we need to save our own soldiers, like what I might be in a couple of years? I would want them to torture that Chinese guy if it would save me. Malcolm shook his head. Torture has been shown over and over to be an ineffective way of gaining information. A person will say anything under torture. Anything. And what they say has nothing to do with with what's true or not. I didn't know what to say to that. Malcolm put the plate of breakfast in front of me. He looked far away for a while, like he was thinking of something else. I ate some of the breakfast. Not the sausage. Then Malcolm said I don't have all the answers, Kyle. I don't think you should be a soldier. I don't think anyone should be made to become a soldier. I just know some things are wrong. And some things are right. Getting you out of the States is right. I said, ok, but now I don't have my own school or friends or town or the places I like to hike, or anything. Malcolm said, that's true, but you can think of it as a grand adventure, Kyle. You are going to a new life. I told him I didn't want a new life. I wanted my old one. But I was starting to understand that wasn't my choice anymore. None of the stuff that happened after I got off the sternwheeler was my choice.

Now I'll tell you more about that. My aunt Thelma didn't say anything for a long time after we ended up on that beach with the shells. We just stood on the sand after the woman in the boat took off into the river again. Finally Aunt Thelma said I guess we need to hike up to the highway. I said we needed to wait until it was morning because we couldn't see anything in the woods. We wouldn't be able to see where we were going. But Aunt Thelma said she wasn't going to wait here in the cold all night. So we started walking up the slope away from the river. There was sand under our feet. I could just see the white spots of sea shells lit up on the sand. Does this mean those people were not really our friends? I said to Aunt Thelma. She didn't want to talk to me. Not because of me, she just didn't want to talk to anyone because it was obvious we were in quite a bit of trouble. But I walked with her into the woods. It wasn't as bad as I thought it would be. We couldn't see much, but we didn't have to. We just followed the slope, walked slowly, tried not to trip on roots or anything.

Then I felt arms around me and a voice whispering in my ear. Everything's safe. Trust what happens next. I heard Aunt Thelma scream a short scream. Kyle? she said. I'm right here, I said. Then another voice. One of the people holding us. The cars are a short distance away, it said. Follow us and say nothing. I thought we were a little bit crazy to be following some people we didn't even know, but we already did that with the boat

                                    Mario Milosevic

when we left the sternwheeler. They led the way around the trees and over a short grassy patch. Then there was a hill we had to climb. It was a little bit muddy and pretty steep. I wasn't sure Aunt Thelma would be able to climb it, and she slipped a couple of times, but the two people leading us pulled her up. They were dressed all in black, and they had black hats on. We ended up in a little clearing off the expressway where there were two cars. One of the people took me to one of the cars, and the other person had Aunt Thelma's arm and was taking her to the other car.

Aunt Thelma said wait a minute. You're not splitting us up. The people stopped. You got a note from someone you know, didn't you? Yesterday morning? Aunt Thelma said yes. What did the note say? Aunt Thelma looked over at me. We were close enough to the expressway that passing headlights lit up her face and I could see the people who were leading us. They were a man and a woman. I know the guy was trying to get Thelma to say the note said to trust what happens next. But she didn't want to say it. Why do we have to split up? she said. I can't let him go on his own. He won't be on his own, said the woman. We've been doing this for a long time. It is best to travel separately because the smaller the group, the easier it is to move quickly. You can get in the car, or we can leave you here. Aunt Thelma said Where are you taking us? Do you know where Allie is? Do you know where my sister is? The people said they only know about this section of the escape but whatever we wanted to happen would work out. They were working to make everything right for both of us. They would deliver us to someone who would take us north. North. I wondered what that meant. I was scared to get into the car, but that note was from my mother and she wouldn't make us go anywhere we shouldn't. Come on Aunt Thelma, I said. She looked like she was going to explode from not knowing what to do. Her hands were twisting around each other. Kyle, she said, I just don't know. It doesn't feel right. I said they don't want to hurt us. My mother wrote that note. If we go with them we'll find her. We'll find my mother.

Then Aunt Thelma takes a deep breath and lets it out real loud. She hugs me hard, harder than anything. I hug her back and I think is this the last time I'll ever see her? I hope not. I just want to go back home where my mother and father are, but they aren't there anymore and I don't always remember that. Sometimes I still think things are the same as they were before. But that's not true. I have to get that through my head.

It's what my aunt Thelma said and it's what Lorraine said and in a way it's what Malcolm said. Then Aunt Thelma lets me go. I'll see you again, she says. Don't worry. We'll find each other. I'm not worried, I say, even though I'm way more worried than I have ever been in my life because where am I going? is my question. Just exactly where is this guy taking me?

So we get in separate cars. The guy tells me to buckle up. We're traveling on the interstate to get around the dam, he says, then you'll get in the river again. As I'm putting on my seat belt he tells me there are sandwiches in the back seat. I'm pretty hungry so I twist around and get the bag. I open it and pull out a sandwich, which turns out to be a fake turkey sandwich and all of a sudden I think that things will be ok, because how did he know I liked fake turkey? Someone must have told him. Someone like my mother or father.

By this time we're going on the expressway, only we're going pretty slow. I tell him he can go faster. He says it isn't wise to go too fast. We don't want to attract attention and get stopped. Oh yeah, I say. How far are we going? About an hour's drive, then we'll put you back in the water. What then? I said. It's out of our hands then, says the guy. The expressway follows the river most of the way. I can see the navigation lights over the water. After a while I see the row of red lights across the river and the lit up tower. That's the dam. We zoom by it. Actually we kind of crawl by it if you want to know the truth. Thanks for the sandwich, I say. You're welcome he says. How did you know I liked this kind, I said. It's best not to know too much or ask too many questions, he said. OK, I said, but you saw my mother right? You know where she is? Remember, it's best not to know too much, said the guy. He turned on the radio and we listened to some talk show about how President Cooper was the best president ever and how she was making the world and the country into the best country it ever was or there was ever going to be because of how she was cracking down on degenerates and subversives. I ask the guy why he listens to this kind of show because when my father was working on a radio show they never would have put this kind of stuff on. Which, I guess, is why he doesn't work at one anymore. The guy says it pays to know your enemy. Enemy. That's what he said. I hated hearing that, thinking we have enemies.

I think I fell asleep. He shakes my shoulder and I open my eyes and we're off the highway, deep in the woods again. It's still dark. I get out of the car and we walk along a path to a dock. I stand at the dock for a while. I see a few boats tied to the dock. Some small outboards and a few sail boats. Which one is ours? I ask. He doesn't answer. I turn around. He's gone. I hear the car's engine start, and the tires crunch over gravel and then I'm alone. I wonder where Aunt Thelma is. Maybe she was right and we shouldn't have been split up. I try to think what time it is. It feels like it must be after midnight. Maybe even 3 or 4 in the morning. It will start to get light soon. Then Malcolm comes out of one of the boats and walks toward me, except at that time I didn't know who he was. He was just some guy from a boat. I think about running, but why bother? I also thought if he wanted to, he could hurt me pretty bad and no one would ever know out here. But so far no one has tried to hurt me. I say who are you? I remember what the other guy said which is that it is best not to know anything. Only this guy tells me. My name's Malcolm, he said. I feel about a million little butterflies in me, all trying to pull me away and my heart is going a million miles a second because he told me his name, so maybe he wasn't one of the people who wouldn't hurt me. Maybe the guy in the car made a mistake.

Or it's Luigi, said the guy from the sailboat. Or maybe it's Harvey. Or Sir Bentley Ashworth. He walked the whole time he was talking. And he was smiling real big, like he was having the time of his life, and I started to relax, like I thought everything was going to be ok. He stopped just a few feet from me. Ever been on a sailboat? he said. I shook my head. What's your real name? I said. It's not Malcolm, Luigi, Harvey, or Sir Bentley Ashworth, he said. But we're going to be aboard my sailboat together for a few days, and Hey You gets old real fast, so I picked Malcolm for now. Is that ok with you? I nodded and we walked to his sailboat.

March 15

I don't even know what to write down first. I'm in a car again, only I'm in Canada. I think we're somewhere in Alberta. Maybe Sasckachewhen. I'm sure I spelled that wrong, but who wouldn't? I mean, come on. Saskashewan. Saskatsciwin. Whatever. We're traveling east. Are you wondering who we is? We is my father and me. Yeah, my father, who three days ago I thought was in jail, but it turns out he was in Canada, plus he was never even in jail even one day. It's pretty incredible and maybe I need to go back to the beginning to tell you the whole thing. So here goes.

After I wrote on March 12, Malcolm told me it was time. I said, time for what? He said this part of the trip was over. I went up the stairs to the deck. We were close to shore. Malcolm pointed. That over there is Vancouver Island, he said. Someone will be there waiting for you who will take you to your next destination. I looked and looked but didn't see anything except trees. Lots of trees. Where's the dock? I said.

No dock, said Malcolm. We're pretty far north to escape the notice of the coast guard and any ordinary folks who might be suspicious. We're at a relatively remote location. We can't land at a real port because the Canadian government allows US representatives to search all incoming boats. I said oh, I didn't know that. So what we have to do, said Malcolm, is get close to shore and let the tide take you in. Oh, I said again. Does that mean I have to get in the water? Oh yes, said Malcolm. But don't worry, I have the tides timed perfectly for you to get safely to shore, and I'm proud to say I've only ever lost a few. A couple of dozen, tops. I look at him and he's grinning like he's the funniest guy in the world, only I'm not laughing. Then he slaps me on the back. When are you going to get a sense of humor, Kyle my man? I told him when the government lets me. I know, lame joke, but you wouldn't know it by the way Kyle laughed and laughed. Good, Kyle, good one, he said. There is much hope for you and your future.

Then he wraps my journal in a plastic bag and stuffs it into my backpack with my clothes and a couple of sandwiches that he made for me. It wasn't much but it's about all I had that was just mine. I'd like to give you a souvenir of your stay on The Sharon, he says, but it's still best to not have evidence of anything, you understand? I nod. Safer for everyone involved, that way. I nod again. I'm feeling pretty sad and I don't even know why. It was fun on the boat. I think when I get older I wouldn't mind having a sailboat. I lean over to Malcolm and just kind of grab onto him. He hugs me back. Good luck to you Kyle, my man. Always remember to hold the spirit of freedom within you. In the end, that's all we have.

I pull away from him and he helps me get into a pair of waders, which are boots that go way up to my waist and there's a ring like an inner tube at the top that wraps around me that I'll float on in the water. Malcolm tells me it will keep me dry and be a life preserver at the same time. What about that I shouldn't have any evidence? I said. He says we'll have to risk it because after all we can't just put you into that cold water with no protection. He puts the backpack on me and we go to the edge of the deck. I got as close as I dare, he says, so I don't damage the keel. Then he helps me climb over the rail and I hang on and feel the water at my feet. I let go of the rail and I fall into the water, which is freezing cold through the waders. Right away I start drifting closer to the shore. Malcolm waves at me. I wave back. Pretty soon Malcolm's boat is getting farther and farther away. The shore looks pretty far away, too, but I'm just supposed to trust the current and the tide to take me in. Trust what happens next is what they've all been saying. But you can't trust completely, because if you did that, then you could get into big trouble. My parents trusted that ART SAVES LIVES, but the art in their gallery didn't save any lives. It turned a lot of lives upside down, is what it did.

At least there weren't any big waves or anything. We were in a bay, so I guess we were protected from all that, which was ok with me. It's hard to say how long I was in the water. It felt like hours and hours, but it was probably more like about 5 minutes. I kept getting closer to the shore so that felt ok. I looked behind me a couple of times and Malcolm's boat was small and getting smaller. Pretty soon he was too small for me to see. Eventually my feet touched the bottom. It felt like gritty sand and then I just started walking to the shore. It was so easy. The shore was a little bit of sand in front of all those trees. I guess Vancouver Island must be all trees with just a narrow ring of sand around it. I wondered if people lived here?

I walked up on the beach. There was kelp all over it, long brown tubes curled up in the sand with some rubbery leaves that looked like miniature palm trees on the end. There were empty crab shells where I think birds must have eaten the crabs out of the shells. The waders felt real heavy all of a sudden. I sat down on the sand and began pulling them off. Then I stood up and looked out at the water. I couldn't see any sign of The Sharon. I decided I needed to go to the trees to hide until someone came for me. I wondered who it would be. I didn't have to wonder for long, because a man started walking toward me from the trees. I figured he must be there for me, whoever he was. I started walking to him.

Once I got a little closer I could tell it was my father and then I ran as fast as I could. He started running too. He shouted my name. I just said Dad Dad Dad about a hundred times. When we got close enough he grabbed me and I grabbed him and we just stood like that on the beach in the middle of nowhere. I wondered if Malcolm knew it was going to be my father here waiting for me, but he probably didn't. None of them knew who it was going to be next. I just had to trust. And I did trust. After a while we stopped hugging each other. I'm so glad to see you, he said. Where's Mom? I said. Is she here with you? How did you get out of jail? And what about Aunt Thelma? Where is she?

He said, All in good time, Kyle. Let's get you off this beach.

He went to where I left the waders and picked them up and then we began walking to the trees. My dad walked pretty fast and I had to walk just as fast to keep up, only I was still cold and pretty tired, so it wasn't that easy. But he slowed down a little to let me catch up. The sand was dry when we got farther from the water, but there was a lot of it and it was hard to walk through it. We walked into the trees and kept walking until we got to a tent and a small circle of stones with a fire. I asked Dad how long he was camped out here. Two days, he said. I wasn't exactly sure when you were going to get here. All I knew is that you were going to be put ashore at this inlet. I asked who told him. He said, that's just it, I never know. I get messages but never know who they're from.

Then I asked where Mom was. Dad said your mother is on her way to your grandfather's. We're going to meet her there. Help me break camp and we'll get going.

So then I wondered do I keep asking about Mom, or do I help with camp? But Dad put out the fire and took down the tent, and rolled up the sleeping bag inside and he wasn't saying much. He handed me a shovel and said dig a hole for the waders. So I started digging. This is so no one knows I was here, right? I said. Right, he said, we can't be too careful. I said even though we're in Canada now? Yes, he said, even though we're in Canada. We are safer here for now, but Canada has its problems too. Being right next to the United States means they inevitably take on some of our characteristics, not always to their benefit. Or ours. Besides, Canada just elected a new government and no one knows if they are going to be more pro US or less so. The betting is they will get closer to the United States because no one wants the US to be mad at them. So we have to be careful.

I said, wait a minute, Mom doesn't like Granddad. My father said no, Kyle, it isn't that she doesn't like him. It's just that they had some disagreements about political issues. That's pretty big, I said. It doesn't have to be, he said. Everyone has disagreements.

Of course I knew that, because even Lorraine and I had disagreements and even Malcolm and I had disagreements, but still, some things are bigger than normal if you have a big disagreement with your dad the way my mother did. Come on, said Dad. I have a car up this way. You can eat once we get going. That was fine with me. I just wanted to be on my way to see my mother. He stuffed some pots and things into my backpack, slung his own pack, with the tent and sleeping bag inside, on his back and we started walking. Dad said how was the trip? I told him about Malcolm, how cool he was to have a sailboat. I told him it was fun but I spent most of my time below decks writing my journal in a log book. Dad said a journal? That's great Kyle. How long have you been doing a journal? I said almost from the day you and Mom got arrested for that ugly art. I said it was Aunt Thelma's idea but at first I thought it was Mom's idea, which is probably what made me want to do it. Otherwise I almost for sure would never have written even one page, let alone however many pages I've done so far. Dad said, that is just fantastic, I'm proud of you, which made me feel good, because then it was like both my mom and dad liked that I was writing a journal. We kept walking. Dad explained what happened that day at the gallery.

After they dragged him out of the gallery, they put him in a car and they were going to take him to the police station, but just as they were about to drive away another cop came up to the car and told the driver he had to go inside because they needed him to help document the evidence. So the driver went back into the gallery and the new cop got in the driver's seat and started driving away. But just a couple of minutes later the cop said he wasn't really a cop. He was there to rescue

Dad from being taken to jail. Dad didn't know anything about this. He asked the guy who he was. The guy said you need to trust what happens next. Then they drove to a hidden place of some trees off the road where there's another car. They get out of the police car and into the other car. The guy takes off the police uniform and they start driving. They don't stop until they get pretty far north and they hide my dad for a couple of weeks, then get him across the border into Canada.

My dad said all this time he was thinking of Mom, wondering what happened to her. I said why didn't they rescue Mom the way they rescued you? He said they tried, but it didn't work. By the time they took Mom out, the cops had figured out the trick. I heard later she put up a good fight, said my dad, which delayed her getting out. What probably would have happened is that we would have been in the same car together and gotten away at the same time, but because she came out later, they couldn't wait for her so they had to get me out of there without Allie. As he was telling me all this I remembered that day, how she was trying to save me. It felt weird to think she wasn't rescued because she was fighting with them and telling me to stay with Aunt Thelma. That took time to do that and that lost time meant she didn't get away with my dad.

Who were the people that rescued you? I asked. I don't know exactly, said Dad. They call themselves patriots. They have an elaborate network that's very complicated. I don't understand it, but I trust them. They saved me, they got your mother away from that hospital after her injuries and they got you here safe and sound. That's good enough for me.

I said, wait a minute, it wasn't injuries, it was a busted appendix. He said, is that what Thelma told you? I said, yes. He said, she probably didn't want to worry you, but it wasn't an appendix, Kyle. Your mother got some internal injuries when she was arrested. She got taken to the hospital because some of those injuries caused internal bleeding. He said this like he didn't want to say it because he didn't want to think it was true. I didn't either. I said, is she all right? I mean about the internal injuries? He said yes, Kyle, she is all right. The network tells me that she actually got good care in the hospital. I wasn't sure if I should believe my dad or not. Suddenly I wasn't sure if I should believe anyone.

I asked my dad how come none of this about him escaping was in the papers. I said everyone including me and Aunt Thelma and the lawyer all thought he was in jail. Dad shrugged.

I guess they didn't want to be publicly embarrassed by how they were fooled so they didn't let the papers know.

It was a lot of stuff to hear. Only I haven't even told you the craziest part yet, but I can't tell it now. It's getting dark here in Sasketchewhen so it's getting harder to see what I'm writing. There's nothing but flat fields of farms all around for more miles than I even thought there were miles. So I won't write anymore right now. I'm feeling sleepy. Dad's driving pretty fast. I guess he wants to get to Toronto too.

March 16

Dad drove all night. We're somewhere near Winnipeg, which is the main city in Manitoba, which is the province beside Ontario, which is where Toronto is which is where my grandfather lives which is where Mom is going to be. Yippee. We're getting lots closer is what I'm saying. It's the morning now and Dad needs to take a nap, so we pulled off into a rest area and he's in the back seat sleeping. I'm going to try to catch up in this journal.

Remember I said there was a crazier part of the story? Here it is. After Dad told me about his escape and everything we were still walking to the car. Only Dad started slowing down. He put out his hand so I slowed down too. I could see up ahead that the trees were thinning out. Dad turned around and put his finger up to his lips. He didn't even say Shhh or anything, that's how quiet he wanted me to be. I could see a car on the other side of the trees. It was parked off the side of the road, which was a dirt road, so I guessed we were pretty far into the woods here. I was surprised there were any roads at all, to tell you the truth. I thought Malcolm had let me off where there weren't any people or towns or anything. Anyway, we went back the way we came, walking quietly to get away from that car. When we had gone quite a way, almost back to the campground, we stopped and my father whispered: I have the feeling there's someone there waiting for us. In a real quiet whisper I said ok, what do we do? Dad said I don't think we can go back to that car. We'll have to hike to the main road. We'll follow the shore for a while, then go inland when we're far enough away from here. I said but we won't have a car. He said I know, but there's nothing we can do about it and we'll have to figure something out later. I said who would be there waiting for us? He said I don't know, Kyle, but we can't take any chances. I said the Canadians aren't after us, are they? He said no, except maybe they were convinced by the American authorities to try to catch him. I thought well this is just great because now who knows when we'll get to my grandfather's since we can't walk forever.

So we start walking along the shore, only not on the sand. We walk where the driftwood is shoved up against the trees where the waves pushed them. We're walking for about ten minutes, I guess, when someone grabs me from behind, putting their arms around me and holding onto me. I yell to my father who is a little way ahead of me since he walks faster than I can keep up. The guy who grabbed me put his hand over my mouth. Even though I'm scared shitless I remember what my mother did so I bite down on the hand pretty hard. The guy screams. I think I know that voice. He lets go of me, I elbow him as hard as I can, then I jump away from him and turn around. It's Les doubled over and grabbing his stomach, and boy, if you think you are surprised, then I was about ten times more surprised. By this time Dad has turned around, dropped his backpack, and is running at me and Les. I take a couple of steps off to the side and then my Dad is right there and he kicks Les hard, aiming for his crotch. Which just in itself is pretty amazing because like I said before, my Dad doesn't even kill bugs, so for him to attack a guy like that is pretty incredible. But Les was trying to kidnap me or something so it's understandable because I totally get that my father was way upset and wasn't going to let Les hurt me. But, see, my dad missed. He didn't quite get Les in the crotch, it was more over to the side, on his thigh. Which meant Les wasn't going to go down real hard because getting kicked in the thigh isn't nearly as bad as getting kicked in the crotch, especially for a guy.

Then what happens is my father loses his balance, I guess because he's not used to kicking people and he falls on his back. So then Les jumps on him and they're on the ground pushing at each other and I'm thinking about when that guy at school jumped on me after I tried to hit him. And on top of that I remembered what Betty said about there has to be a better way than fighting only guess what? I didn't know any better way. If someone is after you, like Les was after me, then just what are you supposed to do? Or what is someone supposed to do who doesn't want to see you get attacked? Can anyone explain that to me? Whoever is reading this, try to come up with a different way and let me know about it, ok? My mother didn't just let those cops take her quietly. She fought back. And don't tell me she did the wrong thing, don't even try to tell me that, because it's like Malcolm said: all we have is freedom and my mom was trying to keep her freedom. That's it. They were trying to hurt her, ok? They made her bleed inside. But anyway, you probably don't want to hear me talk about this. You want to know what happened.

Les and Dad were still rolling around on the ground. I

couldn't tell who was winning the fight. I couldn't even tell if it was a fight at all. Dad was on the bottom, and Les was trying to stay on top and hold him down. Neither of them was hitting or anything. Both of them tried to talk, but they were out of breath and their faces were redder than stop signs. I looked around and found a pretty big branch lying on the ground. I picked it up and walked over to them from behind Les so he couldn't see what I was doing and then I lifted up the branch and swung it down pretty hard on Les's head. He yelled and grabbed his head which gave my father a chance to get out from under him. He crawled away from Les, who let go of his head for a second to try to grab Dad again. But it was obvious Les wasn't going to get to grab Dad because as he reached out Les flopped forward and fell on the ground and he was lying there with his face in the dirt, reaching with his arm, but not getting anywhere.

Now something happened that I can't explain and it scares me, so it feels very important. See, my father was free. He got away. Les was still on the ground. I guess I must have hit him pretty hard and I didn't know if I broke his skull or something. I didn't think so, but I didn't know. Dad said Kyle, come here. Now here's the part that scares me. I looked at Dad and then

I looked at Les and then I lifted up the branch pretty high and dropped it on Les's head so it hit him again. It made a loud clunk, so I knew it was hard and I did it even though me and Dad were not in any danger from Les anymore. Dad said, KYLE! COME HERE. I heard him, but I didn't go right away. I looked down at Les. He was all curled up on the ground. I thought maybe I killed him because there was blood in his hair, but he started moaning so I knew he was alive. I felt like that was probably a good thing. Even though Les was a major jerk that didn't mean he should die or anything. But at the same time I think part of me wouldn't have minded at all if he did die. So that's the scary part. Because no matter who it is, it shouldn't make you feel ok if someone dies. Plus if he did die then I would be in about the biggest trouble anyone can get into. Dad finally runs over and grabs me and pulls me away. I drop the branch and now everything started spinning and I was having a little bit of trouble staying standing up.

Kyle, says Dad, are you ok? I see him, but there are dark patches all around me. I'm seeing him behind clouds or something. My hands and legs are all pulsing, like I've had some kind of drug injected into me. It was weird. And I was scared. Dad asks me again if I'm ok. I say yeah. All he did was grab me and he was just Les. Dad says, you mean you know who this is? I told him he was some kind of security guard who was after me and Aunt Thelma because he said I was a degenerate. And Dad looks so surprised. A security guard followed you all the way from Cedar Falls? That's amazing. And then I get mad at my father and at everyone because we're all in a big mess, and now I've gone and hit someone real hard, which is not good because it's making the mess even worse, and it's like torturing people which is pretty wrong even if you are trying to save lives and stuff. Look, I know it's complicated and no one knows the answer. No one. All I'm saying is I was suddenly mad at the whole world. I just wanted to hit something. Anything. I think I might have wanted to hit my dad. Maybe that doesn't make any sense, but it's the truth. That's what I wanted to do. When I hit Les everything changed. My whole body just went red, the whole world was red. So then after I hit Les those two times I was still mad so I got mad at my father for some reason I still don't get and I yelled at him to stop being such a coward which I can't even tell you where that came from because I have absolutely no idea. And then I started feeling sick. My stomach felt like I ate something rotten and my face got all cold and sweaty. I'm sure you can guess what happened next is that I had to barf. Dad put his hand on my back while I puked all over the ground. He moved so he was between me and Les. I also noticed out of the corner of my eye that Les had somehow pushed himself up so he was sitting. He looked at us. I finished puking and wiped off my mouth. Les put his hand up to his head and pulled it away and looked at the blood. You win, he said. Or something like that. I'm not even sure now. Dad backed away and I backed away with him. All we want is to get in our car and drive away, said Dad. Les waved his hand. Fine, but you won't get far. I'll have the cops on you both for assault. Dad said you don't have jurisdiction here. Les laughed. Doesn't matter. You assaulted me. Get it? So then I said you tried to kidnap me and he laughed again.

Dad bent down and reached into his pack. He pulled out a water bottle and handed it to me. Drink this, Kyle, you don't want to get dehydrated. Then he took out a first aid kit and went over to Les. I opened the bottle and drank some of the water and it was like I was somewhere else watching this movie of my dad bending down beside Les, who I have to tell you looked pretty weird, like he was still stunned, and my dad starts cleaning off his wound and putting a bandage around his head. Yeah, the guy who tried to kidnap me, who tried to fight my dad, who was trying to get us all in some pretty serious trouble, and my dad is taking care of him. It was crazy.

Ok. I hear my dad in the back seat. He's starting to wake up. Maybe the next time I write here I'll be in Toronto.

March 17

First of all, we're not in Toronto, but we are in Ontario. At a garage, because we got a flat tire. It's some city called Sudbury where there are rocks just about everywhere and the biggest smokestack I've ever seen in my life. They do mining here. Some guy in this garage is fixing our tire right now, so I'm writing in the journal. Toronto is only about 250 miles away from here. That's only four hours. Four hours!!! Get it? I asked my dad if Mom was there. He didn't answer the question exactly. He doesn't want to call my grandfather because he's afraid phone calls might be monitored. It must sound like we don't talk much when we're driving but we do, we talk a lot, but it's mostly about stuff you wouldn't be interested in, whoever you are. Because this is supposed to be about how I live my life even though my parents are in jail, only they aren't in jail anymore. So maybe I don't need to write here any more? What do you think, future historian? Should I stop now? For one thing, this logbook Malcolm gave me only has a few more pages in it. If I want to keep going, I need to get another journal.

Maybe I should finish about what happened to Les. I told you how my dad was fixing up Les's wounds and everything. When he was finished, Les looked kind of funny with a white bandage wrapped around his head and his hair sticking up and out all over. I laughed. At first he looked at me like he wanted to kill me, but then something happened. It was crazy, but he started laughing. All of a sudden. It was like someone told the funniest joke in the world about half an hour ago, only he didn't get it until just then and then he couldn't help himself. He just laughed and laughed. So then Dad starts laughing too and after a while I can't help it and I'm laughing with them. All three of us were laughing like we're crazy people, which maybe we were. Les said thanks to my dad. My dad said don't mention it, but could you do me a favor? What's that? said Les. You could tell me who you are and why you were so interested in tracking down me and my son and what you were thinking by grabbing him. Les looks at me. He's still smiling pretty big. I'm just standing and leaning against a tree drinking from the water bottle because I was way thirsty. By this time I didn't feel quite so weird. I didn't feel like someone had put some drugs into me to make me all jittery and stuff. What I'm saying is basically I was a lot calmer. But also I was feeling pretty good, like everything was going to be ok, which makes no sense at all because we were still in the middle of nowhere and Aunt Thelma was gone, and Mom was who knows where and I also had no idea what happened to Lorraine. Les was shivering a little. I guess he was cold, but also he was scared, I think, because it was pretty obvious me and my dad were going to be going soon and he was alone here with a busted up head. Not that I felt sorry for him or anything. I'm just saying what he looked like.

I guess I can tell you, said Les. He looked at me. Remember that pen I gave you? he said. I said, Yeah, what about it? There's a GPS unit in there. I was able to tell where you were from that pen. I couldn't believe that by keeping Les's stupid pen I was telling him where I was the whole time. Les laughed. Don't feel bad, he said. All kinds of people get fooled by that one. Smart criminals and stupid ones. My dad looked disgusted. You put a tracking device on a child, he said. Les shrugged. It was a means to an end, he said to my father. Once I saw Kyle was going out to sea, I was pretty sure I knew where he was going. Kyle had to get out of the country, I figured that out because I figured out you and your wife had to be out of the county, and I have a friend on the force who told me escapees like to come to this part of Vancouver Island. They've tracked other boats to here.

As Les was talking I thought later I would have to let Malcolm know he wasn't as secret as he thought. Only how would I get a message to Malcolm? I also told myself I needed to throw away Les's pen. Les kept talking. He said, so then it was a simple matter of getting to Vancouver Island. I went back to Riverton and took a flight to Victoria, then drove up to here. I saw you had a camp here, so I knew you were waiting for your son. I decided if I waited I'd get both of you.

My dad listened to all of this and then he shook his head. I think I knew what he was thinking, which is that the network was not as perfect as he had thought it was. It wasn't as perfect as anyone had thought it was. Then my Dad asked Les why he was so interested in us and Les said are you kidding? If I can bring you and your wife in then I would be able to quit my job and get a real career in law enforcement. I would be eligible for all kinds of consideration and maybe get out of the security business and into city law enforcement or even anti terrorism squads which is where I can make a mark. My dad said, but we're not terrorists and Les said I don't care if you are or you're not. You might have connections to real terrorists. Besides, the president said you are and that means you're just a way for me to get ahead.

You're not getting ahead here, said my dad. I'd say you got your ass kicked. But you seem to be ok. I don't want to leave you here alone, but I don't think you're in any real danger. You're perfectly capable of walking out of here. I'll leave some water for you. Les nodded his head. Thanks for bandaging me up, he said. Sure, said my dad, we couldn't just leave you with a head wound like that. I know, said Les, but I do appreciate it. I'll just rest here for a while. My head hurts like crazy. You have quite an arm, kid, he says to me. I don't know what to say, because it wasn't my arm that hurt him, it was the branch, which was pretty thick, so I don't say anything. Les is a jerk, no doubt about it, but he didn't seem so bad, sitting there on the ground. He drags himself over to a tree and leans on it. Dad asks him if he's ok. He waves his hand. Get out of here, he says. You have better things to do than worry about me. So that's what we did. We found Les's car parked a ways down the road. He had put some branches on it to hide it. It looked pretty pathetic. My father let the air out of all of his tires. I helped him. I have to say, that was a lot of fun watching Les's car settle down onto the ground. And then we got in my dad's car and we drove away. The rest you know. We drove for a long time because Canada is a pretty big country and now we're in Sudbury. And we're only a few hours from Toronto. They just finished with the car. Here we go.

It's later the same day but we aren't in Toronto anymore. We got to my grandfather's house but it was all dark and empty. My dad found a note under the mat. It said drive to Guelph. Trust what happens next.

So we decide we have to go to Guelph only we don't know where Guelph is. We stop at a gas station where they have a little store attached to it and we get a road atlas and look inside to find out where Guelph is. It's a tiny town way down in south Ontario, past Toronto by about a hundred kilometers, which is something like 60 miles. So that's what we did. We drove to Guelph. We're here now, in downtown Guelph, parked and waiting and I'm on the last page of this journal. I don't know if there's going to be another one because I just absolutely don't know what's going to happen next so I don't know if I should trust anything.

　　　　　　　　　　　　　　　　Mario Milosevic

Book 3

March 18

New journal, and you can tell it's a fancy one. My grandfather gave it to me. He went out and bought about the
nicest journal anyone could find. I think grandfathers and
grandmothers do that sort of thing. They don't just get you
something that works fine, they have to get you something
that works fine but is also leather bound and has a strap around
it so it can close and has the pages all sewn together with
thread instead of glued or stapled and is made from archival
paper, which Granddad told me means the paper will last for
about ten bazillion years. Which I didn't even know that other
kinds of paper has this acid in it that makes them get stiff and
crumbly and they can fall apart in about only a hundred years
sometimes. Which means paper is not always better than
computers. Sure, things written down can last longer, but it's
not that simple because just like electronic stuff, if the paper
isn't archival, then what you write down on paper can be just
as unreadable in the future as computer files because basically

the paper won't even be there.

Which made me think my first two journals were a little bit of a waste of time. They're on the shelf in my room right now. Yeah, I have a room. More on that later. For now, maybe you want to think about what a waste of time those first two journals are as you read this one because this might be the only thing from now that lasts. That means even if you found the other two journals, whoever you are in the future, you maybe can only read this one because the first two fell apart because they weren't on archival paper. If that's what happened, then tough luck because I can't remember everything I wrote in the first book and I'm not going to try.

My grandfather also gave me a fancy pen because that's what grandfathers do, remember? They don't just get you a cheap plastic pen. Oh no. He has to get me some pen that costs fifty dollars, which is just crazy for a pen. I mean, come on, it's just a pen! Only this one is not just a pen. It is made from stainless steel so it's super smooth and heavy in my hand, but not unbalanced like Les's pen was, which I left on the beach, by the way. This new pen has this ink in it that is super black, about the blackest ink that is even possible. I think, ok, it has super black ink. So what? How black does ink have to be? But I told him thanks. Only now I have to be so so so careful I don't lose the pen because it's fifty dollars, which is not ten cents, ok? And another thing is he said I need to be careful about the journal because you don't want the leather to get wet, Kyle, is the way he said it. So now I have to be careful of rain, which I never had to think about with the first journal which was basically just a bunch of papers stapled together and cost 95 cents. The second journal, the log book from Malcolm, was a little better, but not much. It had a heavier cover, but the pages weren't anything special. But maybe I don't have to worry about this one getting wet. Sure, it rains in Cedar Falls all winter, but here in Guelph? I haven't seen a drop yet. So maybe it doesn't rain all that much. Maybe. I guess I'll find out.

All I'm saying is that for a journal and a pen, what I have now is way fancier than it needs to be. Why do things cost more when you have to be more careful with them? Shouldn't it be the other way around? You should pay more for stuff that you don't have to worry about because that way the stuff is way more convenient. Anyway, I guess that's all beside the point because if you're still interested in the story of my life, then you want to know about my mom and stuff.

It's at night and I'm waiting for dinner to get made, which my grandfather is making, and a lot has happened, except not much has happened because we're still in Guelph and I still haven't seen my mother. I'll tell you how we got to where we are.

Remember we were parked in downtown Guelph? We sat there for half an hour or so. It was getting late, almost dark. I said to my dad how long should we wait and he said he didn't know. I told him when we escaped from the sternwheeler we ended up waiting on a shore and we never knew when someone was going to come get us but someone did eventually and he told me that when he got taken on his escape route he was very impressed with how the network seemed to operate so efficiently. I had no idea there were all these people working to protect people like us. I didn't tell my dad I kind of knew about it after Lorraine got away from town because of Betty and Frank. I said will we ever go back home? He said it would be nice but we shouldn't count on it. I didn't like hearing that. I said it's not fair that we have to leave town because of some dumb pictures. He said I know that and then he said he was sorry he and mom put up those pictures because he had no idea any of this was going to happen, but they were tired of not making a difference and they thought an edgy show at the gallery would wake people up, maybe make them not such sautéed vegetables anymore. He said, You know, it was your grandfather who told us about the paintings. He met the artist and liked her work. I think he wants people to stop being sautéed vegetables too. I said I didn't think it worked. Dad said, I know that too and I'm so sorry Kyle. We were very naive and it affected you in a terrible way. We thought we were doing our duty to humanity and the country by putting on that show, by telling the government we didn't go along with some of what they are doing.

I said, you guys always told me it was important to do the right thing and you were just doing what you thought was the right thing. So what if it turned out different than you thought? It's not your fault. It's no big deal. He said, No Kyle, it is important. We were not doing our duty as parents, which is to protect you, and I am sorry for that and I will do everything I can to make sure nothing like that happens again. It was about the strangest thing my father ever said to me. I said it was not his fault that some people got all crazy about some dumb paintings. And he said it was his fault for not seeing where it might have led to. We were kind of repeating ourselves and it was not exactly like he was telling me I was wrong about it not being his fault, but it was like he was saying he was wrong. Which is different, but also the same, in a way, because being wrong is something that happens to everyone, only all the ways of being wrong are not the same, because when the president is wrong she can mess things up for a lot of people and even get them killed. When I'm wrong, like when I dropped that branch on Les the second time, I only messed up one guy's head. Big difference, don't you think? Plus Les deserved it in a way. I'm not saying I was right to bonk him, but I don't feel super bad about it. I mean, I feel bad, but not completely totally bad. I hope that doesn't make me sound like I'm a dangerous person, because I'm not. It was just that one time. OK, and the time I went after that guy at school. But that's it.

Anyway, we were waiting a long time it seemed like, and I was starting to think maybe it was a mistake to come to Guelph, only I didn't know where we were going to go if we went somewhere else and I'm pretty sure Dad was thinking the same thing when we hear a tap on the car window and I'm so surprised I just about jump through the roof. But I look through the window and there's my grandfather grinning at me. I roll down the window. You made it, he said. Glad to see you Kyle. And you, Richard. I said Where's my mom? He told me she was safe and on her way, but he didn't know exactly where she was right then. You've heard from Allie? said Dad. No, said Granddad, but I trust the people that are helping her. They got the two of you here, didn't they?

I thought, Oh great, so after all that driving and trouble, I still wasn't anywhere near my mother. I felt just about the worst I felt during this whole trip from beginning to end. There was even a tiny little thought in me that maybe my mother wasn't even alive anymore, but I didn't think that for too long. Not even for more than about one and a half seconds because I just didn't want to think that was even possible.

My grandfather has an SUV that we all get into. Dad asks what about the car I'm driving? Grandfather says don't worry about it, they'll take care of it. Yeah they. Whoever they is. I was starting to get a little bit mad at the people who were getting us from one place to the other. None of it mattered if my mother was still missing.

Granddad drove out of Guelph. We were in an area with farms everywhere. I think we drove for about an hour. I don't remember exactly because I was in the back seat and I think I fell asleep for a while. The roads were smooth sometimes, then bumpy and unpaved. I was pretty tired. I thought maybe this was going to be where I lived now. Because think about it, I couldn't go back to Cedar Falls and neither could my parents. And we couldn't go back to anywhere in the United States. Plus we couldn't live in Toronto I guess, because that note said it was not safe. So maybe this was going to be my home now. That felt strange, mostly because my mother wasn't around, but also because it was so different from where I used to live and I didn't know anyone here. Plus they probably think Americans are the worst people in the world because the president orders torture and everything and even though I'm not the president and she doesn't order me to do any torturing, I'm still from the country that does. That kind of thing matters, even if it shouldn't. People think things about you just because of where you come from. I thought if I had to go to school here I wouldn't tell anyone where I used to live because I was pretty sure they had guys here who would beat you up if they didn't like you. Why wouldn't they? Guys like that are everywhere. I bet Les was a guy like that when he was a kid. So I'd just say I was from Vancouver or something. They wouldn't know.

So that's what I thought about as we drove. Eventually we

got to this long long driveway. We drove up the driveway and stopped in front of a big house. By this time it was too dark to see much, but I could tell it was a 2 story house with a big porch around it. There were a couple of lights on inside. Granddad parked the car off to the side where the driveway looped around a tree and we all get out. It was cold, but the sky was so big and the stars were brighter than I'd seen them in a long time. It was very quiet. We followed Granddad up the front steps and he opened the door.

So I'm expecting there's no one home, only I'm wrong. There's a woman in the house. She's wearing an apron with paint splotches all over it, and there is a picture on an easel that she is working on. Granddad says Kyle, Richard, I'd like you to meet Margolis. Margolis, this is my son-in-law Richard, and my grandson, Kyle. Dad steps forward to shake her hand. Glad to meet you, finally, he says. I think, finally? Then I notice the picture looks a lot like the ones of the torturing that were in my parent's gallery. I don't mean they had torturing going on, I mean the people in the picture were painted in the same style. So I figure out pretty quick this is the artist who painted the pictures that got my parents in trouble.

Oh boy. Yeah. Once I figure out she is the one who got my

mother into jail I don't want to be anywhere near her or her art. She says to my dad she's glad to meet him too and then she looks at me and puts out her hand. I don't want to shake her hand. I don't even want to look at her. I just turn around and walk away from her and end up in the dining room where I sit at the table with my arms folded up in front of me because I am so mad I feel like when I dropped that branch on Les.

Dad says to Margolis that we've had a long trip and we're very tired. Fine. He can say what he wants. I just want out of here. I don't want to be in the house and I sure don't want to be anywhere near Margolis. Pretty stupid name, too. Margolis. Who names their kid Margolis? She must have had pretty stupid parents, maybe the stupidest parents ever. That's what I'm thinking about the whole time. She's stupid, her parents are stupid, her pictures are stupid, and then I'm starting to think my grandfather and father are stupid for hanging around with her. She says to my father, I understand you've both been under a lot of strain. But you're safe here. You can both rest and get your lives together.

So I say, real loud so everyone can hear, we would already have our lives together if you wouldn't have ever painted those gross stupid disgusting pictures. And you would have thought

I told them all I had a bomb and I was going to let it off if they said another word because suddenly everyone got really really quiet. Including me. I just stared at Margolis. Stared and stared and stared. She had this little smile on her face, like she didn't want to smile but it was something she thought she should do. And then after a long time she says, I'm sorry my paintings led to difficulties for you and your family, but your grandfather told your parents about them and your parents chose to show them. And it's not my fault that your country has a repressive government whose morally deficient policies affect the whole world and which is badly in need of criticism and checking. Yeah, she said all that. She didn't talk like anyone I knew. Even my parents, who must have agreed with her or else they wouldn't have put up her pictures, didn't talk that way.

Now it was weird, because even though I was mad at her I was also mad at my parents, which I already told you, since, like Margolis said, they didn't have to show those pictures. No one made them. They made themselves do it. And because they showed them, here I was in Guelph. Not even in Guelph, but some house outside of Guelph in the middle of nowhere in Canada. So I said to Margolis, don't blame it on the government. They're fighting the Chinese who attacked us, remember? So the government has to do things to protect us. Which I didn't even know I was going to say, but I said it and then Granddad, who hadn't said much up to then raised his voice and said, Come on, enough political talk for now. I'll show you two to your rooms and get you settled in and then we'll have something to eat.

So we go upstairs and my dad and me have separate rooms, which is ok with me because we've been in that car for days and it's about time I got some space of my own. And that's when Granddad gives me the leather covered journal. Leather bound, is what I mean, since that's what he called it. Leather bound, which means made from the skin of some animal, probably a cow. Maybe a sheep. And I ask him where's my mom, doesn't he know anything at all about where my mom is, and I'm about to cry and I'm holding the journal in my hand and I don't want to cry so much that tears fall on it, because he just told me it can't get wet or it'll be completely ruined so I put it to the side, only I don't start crying. I make myself stop. Granddad tells me he read my first journal. He got it in the mail from when me and Aunt Thelma mailed it to him. He said it was one of the most interesting and enlightening things he's ever read and he's glad I wrote it and that's why he wanted me to have a very special place to keep writing my journal. Which all that, what he said, did made me feel a little bit better, but he still didn't say where Mom was. Because he didn't know.

March 19

Margolis is painting my portrait. Right now, while I'm writing in this journal. She says she likes to paint people while they are doing activities characteristic of their personalities and she thinks me writing in journals is very characteristic. I guess that's her opinion. Maybe she's right and maybe she isn't.

After that first time I saw her and told her how mad I was at her, she didn't get mad back at me or anything. In fact, she's actually kind of nice to me. She thinks I'm cool or something. At dinner that first night she asked me about my journal. I said have you read my journal, and she said no because that was private but your grandfather told me about it and I was interested in what motivated you to write it. I said my aunt Thelma said my mother said I should write it, and even though I figured out my mother didn't say anything about me writing a journal because how could she when they wouldn't let her talk to anyone, I still did it to let the world of the future know what was going on in the country. I said if people don't write stuff down, then in the future they won't know anything about us.

She said that's a very interesting point of view for someone so young. I would think at your age you would be more interested in sports and things like that. At least she didn't say anything about skateboards, which was better than Les or Malcolm. I said, what makes you think I'm so young when I could be sent to a war in less than two years? She said, that's a good point, Kyle, but do you know why President Cooper lowered the age of the draft to 16? She said it like I could not possibly know the answer because I was too dumb. I said it was so they could get us before we changed our minds about how great war was because the younger you are the more you want to go. Because when you're young you're kind of stupid and it was easier to make soldiers out of people who wanted to go instead of those who decided war was not so great and they didn't want to go which is what can happen when you get older. Margolis looked surprised. She said, yes, I think that's right, Kyle, and I promise I won't underestimate you again, but what about the world now, Kyle? It's well and good, with your journal, to honor our responsibility to the future, but don't you care about what's going on right now?

And I said of course I do because I don't want to get into a war in two years when I get drafted, but she said I don't think that's an issue now, Kyle, since you are no longer in the States. I said, oh yeah, which made me like her because she told me something that could make me feel a lot better. So that was nice. Then she said that since I don't have to worry about that, then what am I writing the journal for? And she didn't say it like she thought I should stop, but she was just asking because she wanted to know.

Dad and Granddad listened to her ask the question and then they looked at me and all of a sudden I felt like there was a spotlight on me and everyone was expecting me to be brilliant or something. How was I supposed to answer this? I cared about what was going on, sure I did. But the future was important too, wasn't it? So finally I said I never thought I would like to write, but once I got started, and I had this future audience in my head I just almost can't even stop myself. That's good, said my dad. Writing sharpens your thoughts. And my grandfather said, Excellent, Kyle, that's a good answer. But Margolis said being good at something is fine, but what does one do with that talent? That's the important thing. Which made sense in a way. But that just comes back to the thing I talked about before, which is this: What is a kid supposed to do about the world? I mean, come on. And it's not just kids. What does anyone do to fix the world? Especially when the people who are messing it up think they are doing the right thing. Like President Cooper. Everyone says she's becoming a dictator but I'll bet she doesn't think so. I bet she thinks she's just as right as all the people who say she is wrong. So when that happens, who is right and who is wrong? No one knows and don't tell me they do because they don't.

Then Margolis said, I would like to paint your portrait if that's ok with you. I told her my aunt Thelma did a drawing of me that was pretty good and Margolis was going to have to be about the best artist in the world if she was going to do a better portrait than Aunt Thelma did. She said, do you have that drawing? I said yeah, because when we were on the sternwheeler I made sure I kept it. I went to my room and got it out of the backpack. It was pretty wrinkled and creased and stuff and a corner of it got wet before, but you could still tell it was me so I brought it down to Margolis and she spread it out on the table and started studying it carefully, like it was the most interesting thing in the world. I see your aunt is an accomplished artist, she said. This drawing perfectly captures your innocence and your beauty. Yeah, she said beauty. I'm not kidding so don't laugh about it, ok. She's the one who said it, not me. I'm just reporting it. She said See the lines around your eyes and the way she's shaded the chin? I looked at the picture again. I think I saw what she was talking about but I wasn't completely sure. I said, I just like it because it looks like me, that's all. She said, yes, it looks like you, but there's more to it than that. She's captured the truth of you as well. It's clear from this picture that your aunt Thelma truly loves you.

Which might be about the most obvious thing in the world because of course Aunt Thelma loves me. She completely cares about me and what happens to me. Which is why I'm pretty upset that I don't know where she is. Or where my mother is.

Anyway, maybe I'll tell you a little bit more about what's happening here in Guelph. It's the morning. I'm sitting in the living room, in the window. Margolis spent a lot of time positioning me in just the right place for the light to hit me a certain way, which I guess is important to artists. She had me sit in a chair, then she went over to her easel and looked at me, then she had me turn a fraction of an inch, then she looked at me again, then she came over and messed up my hair, even though it was already messed up and had me turn another fraction of an inch. She said thanks for doing this for me, Kyle. I said no problem. Then she said ok, I think I have you the way I can best do justice to the way I perceive you. You can start writing in your journal now if you want.

I picked up the pen and the leather journal my grandfather gave me, which is the one you're reading right now, and I started writing and at the same time Margolis started sketching. She said I would like you to try to keep that pose for about 15 or 20 minutes, Kyle. Can you do that? I said sure. She said because I need to get down the baseline sketch and then I can add to it even though you might be moving around after that point. For this initial phase you can write in your journal, but try not to twist in your chair or anything like that, ok? I said yes. But you know what? It isn't easy to stay in one position for a long time. I'm starting to get tired and my back aches. My neck, too.

Ok. We took a break. She still wants me to pose by the window. The light is changing, she said, but I like you framed there. So fine. I'm still framed in the window. During the break Margolis asked me who I was addressing the journal to. I said I didn't know what she meant by that. She said do you imagine a certain someone reading the journal? Is it like you are writing letters to someone? I told her no. But then I thought maybe I was wrong and I said, well, I do kind of think about some professor person in the future reading it, so I think about what they would be interested in. Also, I think about my mother and father reading it. I want them to read it sometime. But mostly, I guess I want someone in the future to read it. She said that's so interesting, Kyle, that you have the future in mind. Most people only think about the present because that's where we live. It isn't until they have children that they think about the future.

I said maybe I won't think about is so much now that I won't be getting drafted. And then I said, wait a minute, didn't you say you thought people should be more interested in now than the future? She laughed about that. She said it's not an either/or thing. I was just trying to understand your thought processes and what you are about.

She said I'm painting you as part of a series I'm doing on displaced people. She said those are people who have been forced from their homes due to political circumstances. She said there are people like that all over the world. We call them refugees. I said ok, so I'm a refugee? She said, yes, you are. Your circumstances are more fortunate than a lot of other refugees, because you have shelter, food, and family, whereas many people I have encountered in other countries have none of those things. They are literally alone in the world with just the clothes they are wearing, but still. There's something about refugees, that loss, that is so important to document. All refugees share it. It is the shared truth you all carry about what loss means and how to survive when you are confronted with it.

I think I knew what she meant because I do feel like I'm completely in a place I don't want to be and it's because other people made me come here when I didn't want to and there's nothing the same anymore. It's all new. So I'm a refugee. Then she asked me if I was ready to sit some more. I said ok. So now here I am, and she's stopped sketching with a pencil and now she's taken out her paints and she's using a brush.

I didn't tell you what else Granddad told me when he gave me this journal. I asked him whose house this was. He said it was his house that he had with my grandmother. It was where they went when they wanted a vacation from the city. I asked him why they got divorced. He said it was because of his work.

He wanted to help the world but Grandma didn't like what he was doing in the United States to help the government. I guess they must have fought about it quite a bit because as he was telling me about it it looked like he felt pretty bad. He said she ended up moving to New Zealand and becoming part of a religious group that is trying to bring peace to the world. He said she's an admirable woman and I should have seen she was right the whole time, but I waited too long and now she has this other family. He meant she didn't much care about us, her first family, which felt weird, thinking that your own grandmother doesn't care about you, but I was starting to wonder what my grandmother and my mother didn't like about my grandfather so I asked him. I said, what were you doing with the government that was so terrible?

But guess what, he wouldn't answer. He got quiet and he tried to smile at me, but it wasn't a real smile, it was like he was forcing himself to pretend to be relaxed. But he wasn't relaxed at all. He said, I will tell you some day, but not today. So later that night, which was the first night we got here, I asked my father and he said I think your grandfather needs to tell you that. So ok, I'm just a kid and no one wants to tell me, I get it. But let me ask you this, how can I be just a dumb kid now but in about 2 years I'll be old enough to shoot at people from China and have them shoot at me and get me killed? Answer that one for me and I'll give you the biggest medal ever.

Margolis is still painting. She looks like she's slowing down a little though. I think I'm about done writing here for now.

March 20

It's the morning. Last night Granddad and Dad and me went to get my mother. But before you get all interested and everything, we never found her ok? I was about the saddest I've ever been when it turned out we weren't going to see her and I don't know what's going to happen next. But also, I found out what my grandfather did that was so terrible. I'll tell you that later. Just keep reading.

Here's what happened yesterday. Margolis finished my portrait in about three hours. I sat the whole time. I wasn't completely still or anything, because that's about impossible, and if you ever tried it you would understand what I'm talking about because after a while it was like time was going by so slow even though I was writing in the journal the whole time. Margolis put down her brush and said it's finished Kyle. Do you want to see it? I said sure and I closed the journal and went to stand next to her. I don't know how to describe the picture. Maybe it's the future now and you can get on the internet and look it up because later she put it on a website. It's a website that no one can look at in the United States right now because of the restrictions and filters, but maybe in the future you can. Go look it up, because it's pretty amazing. I don't mean because it's me. Even if it wasn't me or anyone I knew, it would still be amazing, because somehow Margolis figured me out. The picture was me in the woods. Yeah. I never told her I like being in the woods, but she knew. How did she know? I don't know. But see, the woods were not just a background, but it was trees and flowers and everything all up in my hair and all over my face, like the parts of the forest were making me. It was just amazing, that's all. Margolis said what do you think of it? I said I liked it a lot better than the torture pictures. She laughed. She said it's certainly more pleasant than the torture pictures. I wanted to do it as a gift to you so I hope you are pleased with it. I'm going to post it to the refugee website, if that's ok with you? I said sure. She showed me the site on granddad's computer, where all these pictures of mostly kids, but also some grown-ups, were that she had painted. These are the human faces of political oppression is what the website said. Then she took a picture of my painting and uploaded it to the site. So there I was, all over the world. I said will these pictures help people? She said that's the hope, Kyle. We want people to see the paintings and be moved by them to take action either politically with protests or monetarily by sending money to agencies that help refugees. I said is this how art saves lives? She said she never thought of it that way, but maybe. I said I didn't need my life to be saved, but I was glad I was on the site. She said everyone needs saving, sometimes.

Then my father came in and said Kyle, we have a message. I said what kind of message? He said we think we know where to find your mother. Want to come meet her? he said it while he was grinning like he knew of course I would say yes, which I said yes right away because I was about as excited as I have ever been in my life. I said, let's go, and we all got into my grandfather's car, except for Margolis. She said this was a family thing and she wouldn't feel right. We were out the door and in the SUV and we drove for about an hour to Lake Ontario, which is a little farther south of Toronto, because my grandfather said he got an encrypted email that said my mother was taking a motor boat across Lake Ontario and we should go meet her. He told me this while we were driving. I was in the back seat. My father was driving and my grandfather was in the passenger seat.

I said how will she know where she is supposed to end up so we can be there waiting for her? Granddad said they have that figured out. They have a landmark that she is supposed to set her eyes on and then she is supposed to go to that spot. I said, will she be alone? Dad said he didn't know. Every escape is different because every escapee has different circumstances. They must have taken my mother to the east coast to hide her because her jailing was pretty high profile and now she had to get across the border. But I said to my dad that he didn't have to go alone when he escaped and neither did I. Going alone sounded way too dangerous. He said every crossing is dangerous. I crossed over land to the north, but it was a remote area and I had help. If no one was there I would almost certainly have gotten lost and probably died. I didn't like hearing that, because it made me think if he could have died then also my mother maybe could die. I said she should not be alone because having help makes a lot more sense than going solo, which is all I'm saying. And Granddad said, we understand the way you feel Kyle. It's just the way things are.

So we drive through a tiny town, smaller than Guelph, smaller than Cedar Falls, even, and we end up at a park. We park the SUV and get out and hike through some woods and down a path, then off the path, and toward the shore. There's a little beach there, and the waves are pretty big. We're at Lake Ontario. There isn't anyone else around. It's just the three of us. We stand there on the sand. Lake Ontario is bigger than I thought it would be. I can't see the other side. Over to the left there's a dock quite a way off. It has a flashing light on the end. I say, is that what she's supposed to row to? Dad says yes. I ask him, are you sure this is a lake? It looks more like the ocean. He says, yes Kyle. I say isn't it dangerous for Mom to go across this? He says yes it is dangerous, Kyle, we've talked about that. He said it like he didn't want to hear anymore questions from me. I guess maybe he was thinking not so good thoughts too, about Mom and everything. He wasn't grinning anymore, that's for sure. Granddad said it's ok. She'll be fine.

We stand there for a long time. I don't see anything on the lake, not a boat or a bird or nothing. Just nothing. The wind is kicking up pretty good. The trees sway. It's cold. I see Granddad hunching his shoulders and trying to keep warm. We wait and wait. Dad tells Granddad it would be ok if he went back to the SUV to keep warm. You too, Kyle, he says. You look pretty cold yourself. I notice my teeth are chattering and I'm shivering. So Granddad and me go back to the vehicle.

We turn on the engine and let the heater warm us up. This is better, says Granddad. I say yeah, this is much better. So we're sitting there, not saying anything for a long time. I say, I sure hope Mom shows up soon. He says me too. Then we don't say anything for a while longer. I say, how come Margolis is staying at your house? He says she needed a place to stay and I admire her work. I said is she your girlfriend or something? He laughs. Nothing like that Kyle, I'm a little old for her. I say, yeah, but you never know so I was just asking. He says you're right, you never know. Margolis has had a terrible life, says Granddad. Her family is from South America. Her parents were killed by her country's government when she was only two. She ended up in Canada where a family adopted her. She's never forgotten where she came from. She likes being at our house, especially when she's in a painting mood. A lot of the time she's traveling to places. She takes photos of people in dangerous parts of the world, then paints them. Her paintings have a powerful effect on people. Letting her stay at the house is a way for me to atone for my sins.

I don't know what that means, but I don't say anything. He stares out the window. Then he says, Kyle, do you know what I used to do? I say I thought he used to be some kind of scientist.

He laughs. Yeah, he says, some kind. I was a psychologist. Do you know what that is? I said it meant he figured out people's brains, how they thought, things like that. He says, that's right, and when people like me, scientists, learn things about people and how they behave, we gain a lot of power and knowledge. We have to be very careful what we do with that knowledge, and to tell you the truth, I wasn't very careful.

I think, ok, finally, I'm going to hear the truth. So I just listen. I don't want to stop him because maybe he won't ever feel like telling me again. My grandfather said, have you ever had the feeling that someone is watching you from behind? I tell him, sure. At school sometimes, in class, when it's really boring. I'll feel like there's a bug in my hair, only it isn't a bug and when I turn around I see some kid has been looking at me because they are so bored by the class like I am too that they have to look at something and their eyes just end up on my hair. It could be anyone's hair, but just by coincidence it ends up on mine and I feel that look.

Granddad says, yes, exactly like that. It's a phenomenon most of us have experienced and a few years ago some researchers who were trying to cure a patient's epilepsy discovered that by stimulating a certain area of the brain, you could duplicate that feeling of being watched. Granddad touched my head just between my eye and my ear and a little bit higher. Right there, he said, is the spot they discovered. It's called the left temporoparietal junction. (If you're wondering how I know how to spell that word, it's because I looked it up later when I was writing this. I also looked up Saskatchewan.) The temporoparietal junction is a special place in the brain, said Granddad. If you get an electrical current sent to that exact spot, you not only feel like someone is watching you, but you get the uncanny feeling that that someone is a duplicate of yourself. It's like a shadow of you is right behind you. And that shadow person does everything you do. If you move your arm, the shadow person moves its arm. If you sit down the shadow person sits down. The effect is quite extraordinary. When it was first discovered, people speculated it might account for the voices in people's heads, or the feeling that there are competing beings inside you, some telling you to do good, others telling you to do bad.

I thought, ok, so far this doesn't sound terrible. I've had thoughts like that. For just one example, trying to decide if I should tell the truth to that woman at the police station or not. So Granddad made people think some things that weren't real. Big deal. But Granddad looked so serious and so almost upset that I didn't say anything.

Granddad kept talking. He said we got a hold of these results and began investigating the effect for ourselves, since it was so fascinating. We used test subjects and determined that by applying different levels of current and slightly different locations of stimulation we could make the shadow person do things differently from the subject. For example, we could make the subject feel like they were being hugged by their shadow person. That was a tremendous breakthrough. It made the subjects feel lots better. We thought we could possibly use the system to help depressed people get better. Then we also determined how to make the shadow person either good or bad. We could make the subjects feel like the shadow person was their friend, or their enemy. We could even make the shadow person tell them to do things. It really was like voices in their heads, just like the early speculation had it. We probably should have stopped right there. Some on the team were very uncomfortable about where the research was going, but I was the senior scientist in charge, and I wanted to pursue the knowledge, so we kept going. After a while we learned a great deal. We got the hang of dancing around in their brains with the electrodes and made their shadow person into anything we wanted it to be. We published our findings and soon after that some official from the American defense department showed up at my office at the University of Toronto with an offer.

I think back on it now, and I should have told them no. But the Chinese had already attacked American bases in the middle east and we were very afraid of world war 3 since it was obvious they wanted Arab oil. If full scale war broke out, if the west could not contain China, then we could all be dead. That's my only excuse, Kyle, for what I did next. I was scared, we all were, so I got seduced. I thought I was doing my part to save the world. I let them recruit me into the American intelligence agency where I was charged with finding efficient ways to get information out of prisoners. I even told myself I wasn't inventing new methods of torture. But I was, Kyle, that's the horrible part, because I ascertained a way to get the shadow person to inflict pain on the prisoners. I figured out how to make the prisoners feel like they had the best friend in the world in their shadow person, and then I manipulated that best friend into making the prisoners feel like if they didn't tell the secrets they knew, they would die the most horrible deaths possible, killed slowly and painfully by their own shadows.

That's what I did, Kyle. That's what made your mother hate me. That's what made me hate myself.

Then Granddad just stared ahead out of the window. I didn't know if I should tell him it was ok what he did, or if I should tell him he was right: he was horrible. I didn't know what to think and I didn't know what to say. If he was trying to save the world, then that was good. But if he was doing horrible things then that was bad. I said when did you stop doing that stuff? He said he only did it for a year, but it was enough. The defense department implemented his ideas and they were still using them on prisoners they captured in the warm war with China. He said he quit that job and went back to Canada. But by that time my grandmother had left him and his daughters totally hated him.

I said, But Granddad, everyone makes mistakes. People shouldn't think you're a bad person because you made a mistake. Which, I know, was a lame thing to say, but if I didn't say something like that, what was I going to say? I know, I could just have said nothing, but sometimes there's a feeling in the air that you can't just say nothing. You have to say something.

Granddad said yes Kyle, you're right. But there are mistakes and then there are *mistakes*. So I guess what he was saying is that his mistakes were like when President Cooper makes a mistake. It was really really big. Then he said I'm telling you what I did so you can understand that your mother has a good reason to dislike me. I don't blame her a bit. I hope she'll come back to me some day, but that's up to her.

I said, I don't think you're bad Granddad. He said go see how your father is doing. I'll wait here. It's cold out there for an old man.

So I went down the trail. Dad was still standing there. He looked at me and I guess he could tell something by the way my face was. He said, he told you? I said yeah and he feels pretty bad about it all. Dad said we were completely surprised when he told us about Margolis and her work, because her paintings were a clear indictment of what he had done. They were saying torture was wrong and what your grandfather did to promote torture was wrong. I said, it was like he was turning the brains of those prisoners into sautéed vegetables, and he didn't even need TV to do it. Dad said I suppose in a way that's true. Then he said, I don't think we're going to see your mother today. I said, I don't think so either.

We waited there for another hour. Then I went back to sit with Granddad. He was asleep. We ended up staying the whole night, taking turns standing at the shore looking for my mother. The rest of the time we stayed in the SUV taking naps. It's morning now. I woke up a while ago and I've been writing in this journal. I'm hungry. I hope we're going to go get something to eat. Granddad looks about as depressed as anything I've ever seen in my life. Ever.

3/20

Thank you for asking me to write in your journal, Kyle. I hope you will read this some day in the future and it will mean something to you, perhaps inspire you to find your true calling, although I would not presume that my words could have that power. I believe any piece of writing is an expression of hope, and it is in the spirit of hope that I accept your invitation to write here.

I am so sorry you live in a world in which war and torture is still going on. That is a terrible tragedy and I believe we should all work together to make such calamities a part of history. I hope you understand that your grandfather, despite his participation in that horror in the past, has become part of the solution and is no longer part of the problem.

My parents were detained and tortured and executed for printing a newspaper critical of their government. This happened when I was just a little girl so of course I don't remember any of it, but the fact that it happened at all still gives me great pain. So I think I understand your own circumstances. And I hope you won't think it presumptuous of me when I say I believe I understand your pain as well. I'm sorry you were not reunited with your mother yesterday, but I have every hope this will happen for you soon. I feel you are angry with your grandfather and I understand this anger. There is nothing wrong with anger. It helps us to understand what is right and wrong and it gives us energy to do the work which must be done. As you pointed out, you are not so young anymore, so I will attempt to speak to you as an adult.

First of all, it is true your grandfather's work has helped to bring pain and suffering to many people, but Kyle, it is important to understand that even when people are caught in circumstances in which they should know better, they don't always do the right thing. This is a hard fact of life that has led to many wars, much death, and suffering on a monumental level. But it is also important to understand that such people, like your grandfather, can recognize what they have done and take steps to attempt to reverse the effects of their errors. That is what your grandfather has done and what he continues to do.

Let me tell you how we met. A gallery in Toronto was

putting on an exhibition of my work. It was opening night. Your parents ran an art gallery, so I'm sure you know how that is: people in elegant clothes, fancy food on trays, everyone holding drinks in their hands and standing around talking quietly. As the featured artist, it was my duty to mingle with the crowd. I met briefly with people, spoke for a few minutes, then moved on. About half way through the night I saw an older man—your grandfather—standing in front of one of my more graphic paintings, one depicting the face of a young woman who had been a torture victim and who had been terribly disfigured by the experience, both physically and emotionally. I could see immediately your grandfather had been through some serious trauma. My work has made me particularly adept at seeing such things in people. I went to stand by him. "I hope you aren't upset by my picture," I said. "My work is really about hope, even though on the surface it might not appear so."

He turned to me and said, "It is very upsetting, but that's not necessarily a bad thing. I may need to be upset."

Well, Kyle, you can imagine there wasn't much room for small talk after such an opening to a conversation. We ended up talking for quite some time. Your grandfather was very open about what he had done in the American defense department. He told me the work he had been involved with haunted him. He felt like he had destroyed himself and destroyed any chance of having a family since his wife had left him and his own daughter hated him. He came to the show as a way to understand his sins. The show, you see, was just a few weeks after he had quit his job at the American defense department.

I will be completely truthful with you now, Kyle, since to do less would be to violate the spirit of honesty such a journal as this should uphold. I found in my heart a sharp and strong hatred for your grandfather. I felt this overpowering urge to either turn and leave him in his misery, or to add to it by striking him. I think what might have stopped me from doing so is that he would have welcomed the pain of a blow and I did not want to give him that relief. But oh, Kyle, I so much wanted to hurt him. I am not proud to say this. By even putting it down on this page, I am admitting to an urge which has led to untold suffering for untold numbers of people. It is precisely what I have devoted my life to trying to halt. And yet, there it was, trying to rise up in me. In fact, the impulses I felt then still give me shame. However, I perceived that understanding those feelings in myself was not separate from my work but an intimate part of it. They were the impulses we must all struggle against.

So I listened to your grandfather as he described his experiments with the imaginary doubles and the ways he was able to use the doubles to torment prisoners into confessions. As I stood listening, I knew at some point in the future I could very well be painting a portrait of someone who had been through a torture session based on the research your grandfather had done.

How did I keep talking to this man, to your grandfather? I cannot tell you precisely. At first I made myself listen to his words, so I could bear witness to evil. But at some point I ceased seeing evil. I saw he was not a bad man. I don't know how this happened. I don't know how I managed to forgive him, but somehow I did. It is a mystery, this blessing of mercy, as many things in life are mysteries: unknowable and deeply comforting.

I am not going to tell you that you need to forgive your grandfather. It is true he has brought great shame to your family, but it is also true he has sought to atone for his deeds. Although I would hasten to add here that this is my perspective. You could have an entirely different view and that is as it should be. All I can say is that through forgiveness I have found the strength to go on with my work and try to bring some sanity to the world.

I think I have written enough here. These are your pages, after all. I truly wish you find your mother soon. I truly wish for you a world filled with love and peace, as I wish it for all people everywhere.

20 March

Hello Kyle. After our long night on the beach, it is good to be back here, in your grandfather's warm house, although I wish with all my heart that Allie was here with us. I miss her terribly, as I'm sure you must miss her as well.

Let me first say I was startled by your request, then a little intimidated. I wondered what I could write here to inspire my son to greatness. What can any father tell his son? Is it even my job to inspire you in such a way? I'm not sure. I have tried to teach by example, not words. We learn by seeing, and we become human beings by doing.

If I had to tell you just one thing, it would be to somehow understand your own true self and honor that in all your words and actions.

I read Margolis's entry. I am humbled by her life and her spirit. She is truly an amazing human being, which your mother and I could see in her art as soon as we were made aware of it. I would read closely her words about your grandfather. I cannot say anything that could improve on them.

It seems you may be angry with all three of us, her, your grandfather, and me. After all, Margolis created the paintings, your grandfather brought them to our attention, and I (with your mother) chose to make them public in our gallery. So we all participated in the events that have turned your life upside down. I regret that, as I have told you. And sometimes anger simply needs time to heal. That is as it is. I am willing to give you that time.

Perhaps it would be best to write about your mother. She is the most important person in my life. My heart has an empty place in it now because I do not know where she is or if she is all right. Even more than the distress I have caused you, this one fact, that she is gone, hurts me more than I can say.

It may interest you to know I originally did not want to display Margolis's work. I thought they were indeed powerful and amazing, but I also thought they were too strong for our little town. I thought they would not be welcomed as art, however provocative, but would be either ignored, or denounced as ugly propaganda. Allie said we had to show the pictures. We had to because they were important to show. Because no other gallery in this country was willing to take the risk. And also because it was her father who offered them to us. I was reluctant to go along with this, Kyle, and I am not now telling you this as a way to blame your mother for the current situation. That is not my intent at all. What I am trying to tell you is that she was the brave one, and I was the cowardly one. Despite what has happened to our lives since the show, I think she was right. Someone had to show the pictures. They made a statement which had to be heard, because if they could have affected just one person to question the horror that is happening in this war with China, that would be enough. One person who, maybe, had the power to change policy or people's minds. That was the intention, Kyle. We were trying to save lives. It may even be that the most important life we saved was your grandfather's, because by accepting his offer of Margolis's paintings, your mother and your grandfather began a path to reconciliation, and I know that has been very important to him, and also very important to her.

I see I have written about the other people in your life, when what I wanted to do was write about you. But what can I say that you don't already know? I love you deeply. I am amazed by the young man you have become and are becoming. I admire your spirit and your compassion. I sympathize with your anguish. Is that enough? I don't know. I hope it is. I am always here for you. I understand sons often find it difficult to be in the presence of their fathers, especially at your age. I try not to take it personally. I think it has something to do with biology, or social conditioning, or the fact that we are no longer a nomadic species, or some other reason that makes about as much sense or non sense. But this will pass as well. We will likely become friends in just a few years. Then we will take walks in the woods together. I look forward to that day.

Thank you for asking me to write in your journal. I hope I gave you something worthwhile.

Mar 20

A day of soul searching and soul bearing, it seems.

First of all, like Margolis and your father, I would like to express my deep gratitude to you, Kyle, for asking me to write in your journal. We share a name, and that fact has given me much comfort over the years. No matter how strained things were between your mother and me, I could always find solace in the fact that she named you after me. I felt our bond was stronger than our separation.

And now, what can I say to you that is worth preserving for the ages? When I was a young parent, your mother and your aunt were my entire existence. I wanted to make the world a place in which they could thrive and live beautiful lives. I cannot say it in any other way. If I had to do anything, then I would do it, no matter what it took, if it meant my daughters were going to be safe and well. I suppose this is what being a parent is all about, and in fact, may serve as a simple definition for the word "parent." I'm sure Alice and Richard feel the same way about you, and that is as it should be. I think back on the man I was then, when your mother was a little girl, and I am startled by the simple power she possessed. She remade my world and I have been transformed by it ever since.

The cruel paradox of life, however, is that you can be blinded by your own desires and lose your way. You can end up doing things which are counter to life and justify them to yourself by saying they are for the greater good. This is how I managed to convince myself that developing efficient methods of torture was a good thing. So no excuses. I was aware of what I was doing, knew the misery it would cause, and yet consented to doing it. I am entirely responsible and would not insult you or this journal by suggesting I was duped or did not know. I knew. I felt guilt and torment the whole time I worked on the project. And yet I continued working on it for a year. I lost my family because of it. Your grandmother fled from me, seeking sanity elsewhere. I believe she has found it and I am happy for her. Your mother refused to talk to me and banished me from her house. Your aunt, out of justifiable and understandable allegiance to your mother, also refused to speak to me. I don't blame them. Your mother marched against the war, she protested against what the United States

                                    Mario Milosevic

government was doing, and by extension, what I was doing. This was hard to see, but something I had to see. It is what eventually made me turn away from those activities. Seeing that my daughter—your mother—had a sharp and unerring eye for what was moral and what was not, is, more than anything else, what made me quit the project I was involved with. So even though she could not bear to be in my presence, I have deep gratitude for her example.

As you know, my professional life has been devoted to understanding the workings of the human mind. I spent years in that pursuit. I learned a few things, but, on balance, I learned nothing of any importance. It was all just tricks and trivia. What I should have been doing all that time is understanding the human heart. Your mother helped me begin along that path. Margolis has helped as well.

I understand you feel anger toward me. I sense a certain wall between us, but that might be because we have not spent much time together. I won't try to analyze too much. Just, please, if you can, learn from my mistake. Stay true to life. Stay true to your own heart.

March 20

One thing I can tell you is this is a long day and I've learned a few things. For example, police stations are pretty much the same in the United States and in Canada. The officers wear different uniforms, and the furniture is a little nicer here, but the attitude is the same and the way they look at you like they *expect* you to be some kind of criminal without even knowing a single thing about you is the same. I'm waiting here with my Dad. Let me tell you how we got here.

When we got back this morning from waiting at Lake Ontario, waiting and never seeing my mother, which seems like years ago, but was only about 14 hours, I thought, well, this is it. We can't just wait around here forever. I asked Granddad to find out what happened. He said it doesn't work that way, Kyle, they contact us, we don't contact them. I told him that was stupid. He said I know it's hard, but there isn't anything we can do. I told him he probably didn't even know what he was talking about since he figured out how to torture people, that was his whole thing was how to torture people and didn't that make him feel good about himself? Yeah. I said all that even though I know he doesn't feel good about it anymore, if he ever did. But I didn't care, because no one was *doing* anything about Mom. No one. Not even me, ok? But what was I supposed to do? Granddad was the one who could talk to these people. He was the one who got us here, or at least got other people to get us here. Dad was way upset about what I said to Granddad. He said, Kyle, that's no way to talk to your grandfather, but that's not what Margolis said. She said it's ok, Richard, he needs to express this. Which didn't make my dad very happy. He looks at her like he wants to kick her out of the house. But she was right, ok? She was right that I was allowed to say what I wanted to say, and it didn't matter if it made other people mad because, here's the thing: NO ONE KNEW WHERE MOM WAS. So I did some more expressing. I said who did he think he was messing with people's brains and didn't he feel like about the worst guy there ever was in the world and where was Mom, huh? Where was Mom? Why wasn't she here? Just answer that for me, will you? Where is my mother, mister torturer? Where is she mister smart scientist guy who knows everything about how to torture people and invents new ways to torture like he's oh so super duper rocket scientist smart.

And Granddad just looks straight at me and he says Kyle, can you tell me something? I say, what? He says, how did it feel when that branch landed on that man's head? How did that make you feel? Now, ok, I can see what he was doing. He was mad about me calling him a torturer and he was tired of me, so he said something he knew was going to upset me big time. Plus, he's a brain scientist and all, so he could find the one thing pretty quick, and oh boy, he was right. Because I was still feeling bad about hitting Les. It still felt like the worst thing I ever did. But I didn't want to think about it too much right then. So I said F you Granddad. Just go F yourself. Only I didn't say F. I said the whole word.

So then, just like before, they all got quiet and I felt like none of them knew anything about anything that mattered. But neither did I. I knew less than nothing. I didn't know where my mother was. I said and what about Aunt Thelma? Where is she? And Lorraine? My best friend and I don't know where he is? You think this network is some great thing, but all it did was get Dad and me here and what good did that do? Even a dumb ass like Les figured out your stupid network.

I went on like that for a while. They just let me rave on. Maybe they enjoyed it. Maybe it was like theater for them. I don't know. After a while I got tired of it and I stopped talking. Margolis came over to me and hugged me. Just grabbed me like I was her own son or something, and normally I think I would be embarrassed by that but not this time. I kind of fell against her and let her hug me. She felt like my mother. I closed my eyes and I think for about half a second I believed she *was* my mother. I'm 14, which I know you already know, but just then, right at that time while Margolis was hugging me, I felt like I was only 2. I felt like a little kid who didn't know anything and it felt good. It felt right to be that little kid because even though babies are completely ignorant about everything, they sure are happier than people who aren't ignorant. Then she let me go and I'm not crying, which is what I thought would happen. She asks me if I feel better. I tell her yes. She says it's hard for everyone. Isn't that right? She looks at Dad and Granddad. They both say yes. We don't want any of this to be happening, says Granddad. But you know what? I can't look at him. I feel like there's something wrong with him. Even though he's sorry, it isn't enough.

Dad says, how about some breakfast? Margolis says I think

that would be a good idea. Then we all end up in the kitchen. Margolis tells everyone what to do. She has me get eggs from the fridge. She has Dad make toast. She tells Granddad to set the table. And then it all seemed normal again. People weren't quiet anymore and we started talking. I said I remembered when Mom would make breakfast. Her pancakes were so good. And Granddad said I showed her how to make those pancakes. Which was funny, because I don't always remember Granddad is Mom's father. I know, it's so simple, but it sometimes just is not there in my brain. I can't explain it.

Then we all sit at the table eating breakfast and Granddad asks me how the journal is going. I tell him I write in it, but I don't know if it does any good. He says think of it as a record of this time, Kyle. Think of it as history. I tell him I do think of it as history because I think about some future professor reading it and going Oh wow, is that really what happened then? but I still feel like I don't know enough.

Granddad said don't worry about it. You know plenty. It's about you, and who knows more about that subject than you do? So then I got this crazy idea. I said since you are all the grown-ups who are trying to save the world and everything and you are doing a lousy job of it if you ask me, why don't you all write something in my journal, which will last forever so anyone in the future will be able to read it and see just how smart you are?

Maybe you've felt crazy in your life. Maybe not. If you never have then you are lucky and I wish I was like you, because right then, I felt as crazy as I have ever been in my entire life. But here's the funny thing. They all said yes. They said, what a great idea, Kyle. We'd be happy to. Actually that's what Margolis said. Dad and Granddad looked a little nervous but they nodded and said, yeah Kyle. We'll do that for you. Maybe they were just trying to make me happy or something. I don't know if they wanted to do it, but they said they did, so I gave the journal to Margolis.

While I waited for them all to write in it I went to Granddad's library. He had a lot of books about psychology which looked extremely boring. Except I wondered if they had sections in them on how to torture people mentally. I thought maybe that's where Granddad got the idea. I didn't open any of them. There were books on history which looked a little more interesting, but not much. I knew what history was. It was wars and disasters and stuff like that. I didn't need any of those books. I looked and looked, but he didn't have much I would call fun. So ok, Granddad is not a fun guy. I thought of Betty and Frank's library, how it was stuffed with books I would want to read. Now here I was in a big house with a whole room that was a library, and I didn't see a single thing I wanted to read. There were cookbooks on one of the shelves. I pulled down a big one, which just happened to be a vegetarian cookbook. I thought, huh, Granddad must be a vegetarian, I guess. So I looked through the book. It had some pictures of food. There were recipes. Some of the recipes I recognized because my mother has made them. So then I thought maybe this book is where she got the recipes from. And maybe she is vegetarian because Granddad is vegetarian. I don't know how to describe what happened next, except it was the kind of thing that makes your head sort of turn upside down. That's what it felt like. I suddenly realized Granddad was my mother's father. OK, I know that sounds stupid, and maybe it is, but it isn't like I suddenly knew something I didn't know before. It was more like I suddenly felt something I didn't feel before. Maybe you're reading this and you think what is he talking about? I would probably think the same thing if I read something like this. But they were all in the other room, writing in my journal because I asked them. Everything was different. I saw things I didn't see before. Or I thought I saw them. I looked around the room, Granddad's library, and my head was exploding. That's what it felt like. My head was not as small as it used to be. I looked out the window at the green fields. I wanted to see my mother walking through that field to this house. I saw a bird fly over the field. I saw the sun moving across the sky. I saw everything. And at that moment I was sure my mother was never coming home. I was so tired and my hope just ran out.

Then I think I must have fallen asleep because the next thing I know, Dad is shaking my shoulder.

Kyle, he says. We got a call from the police. They have your mother.

So now you know how I got here. I'm at the police station, in this little area near the desk where a cop is standing like he's guarding President Cooper or something and where there are a few chairs we can sit on and wait to see my mother. So we're waiting. And waiting. Dad is sitting right beside me and he's about as upset as I've ever seen him. He's gone to the officer about five times and asked where Mom is. They keep telling him to go back to his chair and wait quietly *please*. They say *please* but they don't mean it. Margolis is here too. She holds my hand sometimes as we're waiting, mostly because I grab her hand and she's a nice person so she doesn't let go of me. We're waiting to see my mother, I hope, but you never know. Things have absolutely not turned out the way I thought they were going to. I don't trust what's going to happen next.

You may be wondering where Granddad is. I won't keep you in suspense forever. He's in jail. They are saying he is a war criminal.

March 21

It's after midnight. We're still at the police station. It takes a long time for them to do things. Here's what I know from what the officer at the desk told Dad.

Mom got off course. She ended up way farther east from where we were waiting for her. She was following a light, like she was supposed to, but it was the wrong light. So she ended up on the shore. That's why we didn't find her. When she landed she wasn't near any city or park or anything. She pulled up the boat and then she waited. Because they told her someone would be there. That someone was us, Dad and Granddad and me. After a long time waiting, she figured out something was wrong and she started walking inland. Remember, she didn't know exactly where she was, but she saw a house and she went to knock on the door and ask them if she can use their phone to call Granddad. The people let her in and gave her a phone. While she was trying to remember Granddad's phone number, the people in the house called the cops on another phone. So much for helping out strangers in distress, huh? So while she was there in these people's house the cops came and took her away because she had no papers or money or anything and even though she told them she was Canadian, they didn't believe her I guess, and they took her in. I think, ok, she doesn't have any papers because she's running away from being in jail in another country, so now she gets to her own country and they decide to put her in jail? OK. Makes sense to me.

I'll get to my grandfather in a minute, in case you're wondering. Did I mention this is a long day? Brace yourself, it isn't over yet.

So at the police station where they take her, which is where we are now, she tells them to call Granddad so someone will come get her because she is a Canadian citizen, not a foreigner. It isn't exactly that they don't believe her, but it's more that they have these procedures they have to go through because even though she says she is supposed to be living here, she looks like someone who has sneaked into the country. So they get a hold of Granddad to come get her, which is when my dad woke me up in the library, and we all went down to the police station, and guess what. They told us Mom will be processed and released, so we were all pretty excited about that, but then they grabbed Granddad and told him he was under arrest for crimes against humanity. Yeah. Crimes against humanity. I didn't even know there was such a thing as crimes against humanity, but there is. And Granddad will have to go to court and be tried. So according to the Canadians, Granddad is about the worst criminal there is, because he didn't just do something against one person, he did something against the entire population of humans. You don't have to know another single thing about it to know that has to be pretty serious.

So when this happens, Granddad looks happier than I've ever seen him. Margolis tells him not to worry. They will work to get him released. Granddad doesn't say anything as they take him away.

I tell Dad, we can't let Granddad go to jail. He says there isn't anything we can do. I said, but he's different now. He's sorry he invented new ways to torture. He's sorry, he's sorry. Dad says I know, Kyle, but there's nothing we can do. I said we need to find a lawyer. They can get Granddad out. He said we will find a lawyer, but it's late now. We'll find one in the morning. I said NO. We have to find one NOW. Dad just shakes his head. We don't need any hysterics now, he said.

Your mother will be out soon. Then we can decide what we need to do.

I guess he was right, but that didn't make me feel any better. I felt sick. Margolis said, you know, I think he may have wanted this for a while now. I said that's crazy. No one wants to go to jail. No one wants to be a criminal. She said, of course not, Kyle, but he feels like he has unfinished business. This may be the punishment he needs to find his own peace.

If you have been reading up to now, you know I spend a lot of time trying to figure out what grown-ups say and why they say it and what it all means. But I have to tell you, what Margolis told me, I just don't get it in any way at all.

Like I said, this has been a long day. My mom still isn't out, but they say she will be soon. I'm too tired to write anymore.

March 21

Mom's back home. Or, at least she's back at Granddad's place, which is the closest thing to home we have now. I never saw her come out of jail. I was asleep. It's not my fault. It was such a long day that I couldn't stay awake anymore. I was asleep and then I hear this whisper in my ear. It's my mother's voice, saying my name. I thought I must be dreaming, but I wasn't. I opened my eyes and there's my mother. Her face is big in front of me. She is smiling as wide as she has ever smiled. Where have you been? she says, real soft, like she's afraid if she talks too loud she'll break me or something. My father is standing behind her. He has his arm on her shoulder. His eyes are wet. I reach up, like I'm trying to grab the sky, and I hold onto my mother for a long time. She doesn't let me go. I don't even say anything and neither does she. I think I have to hold on for so long because I have to convince myself she is real. She is my real life mother. After that we leave the police station and drive back to Granddad's.

Now it's the afternoon. I slept late, after staying up with Mom and Dad and Margolis most of the night. They were all trying to figure out what to do about Granddad. I thought maybe Mom would want him to rot in jail because she hated him so much. That just goes to show you how much I know, because she only wants to get him out. She kept saying how could this happen? How could they take him just like that? This is supposed to be a better country than the States. We are supposed to be more free. But Dad kept saying the new prime minister was trying to make Canada more independent of the US so they are prosecuting people who have contributed to the war against China if they did things against the Geneva convention, which is this list of rules people have to follow when they fight wars. Have you ever heard of anything more crazy? Maybe you have. But not me. Rules about how you're supposed to kill other soldiers in a war? That's just nuts. Like suppose I'm in a war and I kill some Chinese guy the right way, then I kill another Chinese guy the wrong way. What difference does it make? Aren't I supposed to be there to kill them? That's sure what I thought. But the Geneva convention is about more than just that. It's also about how you treat prisoners and civilians, who are the people who are just living where the war is but not actually a part of the war. So it's like they all know war is wrong and everything because they made up this list of rules that you can't do certain things, except those are exactly the kinds of things that happen in war so having a list of rules doesn't even make any sense whatsoever.

But anyway, one of the rules is you don't torture people. And even though Canada isn't in this war with China, they feel like my grandfather broke that rule, which, you can't disagree with that, because even he said what he did was wrong and he shouldn't have done it. So I guess he's in pretty much of a bad situation. Mom and Dad talked about it all night, talked about what they should do and how they should help him. They said they thought the best way to go would be on the grounds that Canada has no jurisdiction in this case because they are not involved in the war so they cannot prosecute violations of the convention. I guess lawyers will have to figure that one out for sure. They asked Margolis if she knew any. She said all the lawyers she knows would probably jump at the chance to prosecute Granddad and they would do it for free. She didn't say it like a joke or anything, but everyone laughed at it anyway. I said, that's not funny. Mom said, I know Kyle, but we're all very tense and upset. A little black humor can help with the stress.

Maybe with their stress, but not mine. Dad said this will be a high profile case. We might be able to find a lawyer who wants to make a name for him or her self. Mom said that would be a good avenue to explore.

Now remember, all this is happening in the middle of the night after we got home from getting Mom from the police station. We're all waiting for the morning so we can start calling lawyers. Mom says you might want to go to sleep, Kyle. We'll take care of this. I say but I don't want to go to bed because it feels like big things are happening and I would miss them all. Then I say you know what? I'm just as bad as Granddad so maybe they should put me in jail too. She says what are you talking about? And I tell her about how I hit Les when I didn't even need to. Which, I'm telling you right here, was about the hardest thing I ever had to tell anyone, because my mother believes so completely in non violence. She said It's ok Kyle. We all do things we regret. The important thing is to learn from them. What did you learn from your attack on that man?

I told her I didn't learn anything except I had to throw up. She said that's because bringing physical harm to another human being is a stressful thing to do to yourself. It's not a natural action because a human being's instincts are to protect others, not do them harm and you reacted like you had been violated yourself. I said oh. She said what else did you learn? I said nothing. She said you're not trying Kyle. You need to consider the question carefully. You need to understand what you did and why you did it.

See, I didn't want her to say that. I wanted her to say good for you Kyle. Good for you for hitting that jerk of a guy. He deserved it. Which doesn't even make any sense because I already knew she was against hitting people. But I still wanted that. I wanted her to say that because then it would make me feel so much better. But she was still wanting me to think about things. She was gone all that time, and now she was back and everything was all back to normal in a strange way in about three minutes flat. It was like she was never gone.

I said to my mom, is your internal bleeding better? Because I would sure like to take a big branch and break open the skulls of the guys who did that to you just to teach them a good lesson and I wouldn't even care if it made me throw up because that only lasts for a minute or so and after it I would be just fine but they would still have cracked open skulls. I think I said that because I knew she wouldn't like to hear it. I think I was trying to make her mad or something. She looked so surprised. And even a little bit sad. She said I don't want to hear talk like that Kyle. My injuries are my own business. I made the conscious choice to resist arrest and I knew the possible consequences. You are not to avenge me, do you understand? You do not have that right, Kyle, nor do you have my permission. I will not grant it to you.

My face felt hotter than fire, but I said ok. She said I'm not kidding, Kyle. I don't want you taking up arms for me or for anyone else, do you understand? I said ok ok, and I thought how could this happen? How could I want my mom back for all these weeks and when she gets back it's not right at all because it's like she's mad at me. It's like we're different and she maybe doesn't even like me anymore and I'm not even sure I like her the same way as I did. It's just all messed up is what I'm saying.

But anyway, Mom and Dad just weren't interested in me last night. They just didn't much care about me because I wasn't in trouble. I was right there in the house with them but Granddad was not. So they kept going over what they should do about Granddad. And you know what? I don't want Granddad to die in jail or anything and I don't want him to even be in jail, but sometimes things happen. Like when Les came after me. He got what he deserved. And maybe, after Granddad invented all those new ways to torture people, maybe he got what he deserved too. Maybe maybe. I don't know. They said all along we should trust what happens next. Well what happened next is they caught my grandfather. While we were supposed to be doing all that trusting, they came and got my grandfather and there isn't anything anyone can do about it.

March 22

Mom and Dad got a lawyer. She's supposed to be a pretty good one. She's worked on other cases where she has defended people in other countries that have done some pretty bad things. Dad says she's just the kind of unscrupulous and amoral person they need right now. I guess that's more black humor or something because Margolis and Mom laughed when he said that. I'm not ready to laugh about it. Mom said oh, come on Kyle, you have to lighten up a little. I told her that's what Malcolm said. I said does that mean I'm just too serious? She said you aren't too anything, you're just right. Then she asked me what it was like on the sailboat. I told her it was fun and then we started talking about it and then everything was better. She read all my journals. She said they were very well done and Aunt Thelma was right, it is just the sort of thing she would have asked me to do.

Margolis is gone. She said she had to go to where the fighting is going on with China and the United States because there are a lot of people who are being displaced from their countries because they have to get away from the fighting. She's not going alone. There are a group of them, writers and photographers and people like that who are going to document the refugees. I told her to be careful. She said I'm always careful, Kyle. I think she said that to make me feel better because I'm pretty sure she does a lot of dangerous things to get the pictures she wants. I said I'll look on the website to see your paintings. She said, thank you Kyle, it makes me feel very proud that you would want to look at my paintings. She said it like I was some important guy or something.

We got a letter from Aunt Thelma. It was in the mailbox for a while because there was so much going on here that no one thought about looking in there, plus first it went to Toronto and then it had to be forwarded here. The letter was for Granddad, but Mom opened it because Granddad isn't here, obviously. Then she let me read it. I'll just paste it in here so you can read it for yourself and I won't have to describe it.

3/12

Dear Dad:

I've tried phoning, but I guess they're onto us. I can't get through to you. In fact I can't make any long distance calls at all. So I'm caught up in all this just as much as the rest of you. I know you wanted us all to be there in Canada with you. I hope Kyle and Dick are with you now or will be soon. I can only assume Allie is on her way too, and of course I hope that happens. But for myself, I have made a hard decision. I have chosen to stay here in Cedar Falls.

Not that I didn't think of running away, I did. I felt like my life came to a crossroads on that shore on the river after Kyle and I left the sternwheeler. I knew he had to get out because Allie and Dick had to get out, and he needed to be with them. But for me it was different. After they split up Kyle and me, I told the person driving me to take me back to my home. I have built a life in Cedar Falls and in this country, and even though this country is not what it used to be (I have heard that phrase so many times in the past few weeks, mostly in my own head) leaving it won't make it any better. We can't all run away from our problems. It is simply not practical for everyone here to cross the border into Canada. I know this country has lost its way, somehow, but it can still stand for something if there are enough people to care, and I still care. There is still much to fight for and that's what I'm going to try to do.

I think the hardest thing I ever did in my life was letting Kyle go. It was such an exercise in faith. I had to trust completely in a process I knew nothing about, and that does not come easily to me. But I had the note from Allie, and I suspected you were part of the plan too, so I made that hard decision to simply—let go. I know from another source, a man named Les, that indeed Kyle did get away safely, and so did Richard. In fact, Les says Kyle knocked some sense into him. I'm sure Kyle will tell you that story when you see him.

Let me tell you a little bit about Les, and then maybe you will understand my decision a little better. He is a simple man, who had grandiose ideas of glory. He regrets this very much and has apologized for his actions, specifically how he tried to use a relationship with me to get information about Allie and Dick. I know, it sounds awful, and it was awful. He was willing to put all of us in danger for his own gain. But. And this is a big but. He says when he was on Vancouver Island Dick helped tend to his injuries. This simple act of kindness made him realize a country which incarcerates and forces to leave such people as my brother-in-law and his family has some big problems of its own, problems that need to be addressed. What that means, exactly, he doesn't know yet, but upon his return to Cedar Falls, the first thing he did was look me up and express his heart felt apologies to me and to Kyle. I was prepared to tell him to go to hell, but there was something in him that seemed different, like he really did have more sense, so I agreed to talk to him, and it turns out he is not such a bad man after all. He simply lost his way for a while. I truly believe he is a changed person.

The funny thing is, Les does know people in the police force and when the trailer of this old couple with all the forbidden books in it mysteriously burned to the ground a few nights after Les returned, there was no evidence against the couple so he called in some favors and got them released. I don't think I have ever been more proud of anyone as I was then. It is too bad that all those books had to be burned for that couple to gain freedom, but you know, I understand sometimes you have to destroy to save. It's a hard lesson for anyone to learn, but Les taught it to me, and I once thought that I could never learn something from a man like Les. I told him he was thinking globally and acting locally and that was a fine thing to do. I'm not sure he understood what I meant, but he was pleased that I was proud of him. With the insurance money the couple got from the trailer, I found them a nice little house near the river and we have already helped them to get set up. Les and I are friends now and it feels good to have someone like him on my side. I don't know what we are going to do next, but whatever it is, I know it will make the family proud.

Dad, I just want to say I never hated you. I was very disappointed by your decision to work for the intelligence department, but I was deeply sorry for you when Mom decided to leave you. That was not something I expected to happen. I miss her too, and wish she had never run away, but everyone has to do what they think is right. I suppose it was much easier for her to leave knowing Allie and me were grown up with lives of our own.

What I hope is that the world will be a better place and that we can help make it so.

With all my love,

Thelma.

Mom said she was glad to hear Betty and Frank were ok. I said I was happy too, but I didn't like that Aunt Thelma stayed in Cedar Falls. Was I ever going to see her again? Mom said I might want to write a letter to her to let her know how things were going for me. I did that and I already sent it. It was hard to write, though, because I was thinking of Granddad the whole time. I wish I was old enough to go visit him. I want to talk to him. I want to tell him what he did was pretty bad, but that doesn't mean he's the worst person in the world. He was just a guy who made a mistake. That's all. He just made one mistake.

Book 4

April 19

Thelma gave you a journal, Kyle, then Malcolm and your grandfather. So now I guess it's my turn. I'll put this in your back pack next to your lunch when I've finished writing in it so you will find it during your trip north.

I can hardly imagine a worse thing in my life, Kyle, than sending you away to where you are going now. I have worked all my life to keep young men like you from making the decision to take up arms, and even though I know you are not exactly doing that, it is the next closest thing. So here is this brand new journal for you to record your thoughts, and, hopefully come to some sense of what is important in life. Of course you have to make your own decisions, but I don't have to tell you what I think the right decision is here.

I will make this entry short so you can tear it out if you find you absolutely cannot stand having these words from your mother in it. But I hope you won't. The only reason you are going where you are going is because of your father. He thinks you need to start making your own decisions. I hope he is right.

Remember what I told you before. Violence is not a natural thing. We are not born to it, and we do not wear it well. It violates our true nature and causes destruction and heart break wherever it is deployed. I hope you will learn this. I hope you will shake off this terrible need you seem to have to prove something. You never have to prove anything to me. You only have to be who you are.

April 20

Please excuse the shaky writing. I just read what my Mom wrote and now I'm writing in this new journal. I'm on a bus, on my way to the Canadian army's early recruitment program way up in Northern Ontario. That's where they have kids like me tromp around in the woods for a couple of weeks learning survival skills, how to trap and eat small game, how to handle firearms, how to take orders, and generally getting ready to become soldiers. It's probably going to be cold and miserable. Outside the window I see patches of snow still on the ground, and we still have a couple of hundred miles to go, so I'm sure where we end up will be a lot snowier and a lot colder. The program is a good way for kids to decide if they actually want to join up when they get old enough. Spending time in the woods I think I will like. The soldier part, I'm not so sure about, but I guess being a soldier is not something you actually *like*, necessarily. It's more something you do out of a sense of duty. I'm going through the whole early recruitment program, even though I'm 99% certain I know what my ultimate decision about becoming a soldier is going to be.

So this is the first day in a new journal. I'm still not writing it for myself. I still think about some mythical academic in the future finding this and using it for research. As it happens, the first three journals I wrote are now gone. The authorities came to the house and took them for evidence in the trial against Granddad. It hurts to know some of what I wrote in there might be used against him. I think I remember early on, perhaps even on the first page of the first journal, I thought I might want to burn them at some point. In retrospect, I suppose I should have. For my grandfather's sake. But that's a moot point now. I didn't burn them. The authorities have them, and preparations for the trial are getting underway. Mom says it will probably be some time in the fall, but there's no telling. It looks like he is most likely going to be found guilty. Mom and Dad don't exactly say that, but I can tell by the way they talk that it looks bad. I suppose it's possible he will win his trial and get out, but I'm not counting on it. Granddad's lawyer is doing her best to delay the proceedings. If convicted, his crimes carry a life sentence, with no possibility of parole. Just writing down those words are hard. How can my grandfather be in such a predicament?

Before the cops took the journals Mom and Dad both read them all the way through. I guess I would have liked Granddad to read them, but it looks like he probably won't.

Me and Dad are Canadian citizens now. It's mostly because Mom is a citizen, and we were fleeing a repressive regime. Both those facts speeded up the process considerably.

We had to leave Granddad's house. Mom and Dad sold it to get money for the lawyer. We ended up moving to Toronto. Dad works at a small art gallery. It doesn't display much in the way of political work. Mostly landscapes and pretty portraits. I guess after what we've been through, he feels like some gentle beauty is welcome and that seems right. Art can save lives, isn't that what Mom always said? Maybe it's saving my father's life. Who knows. Mom could have worked there too, but she found another job. She's working as an advocate for refugees who come into Canada seeking political asylum. I'm sure you will have guessed that neither of these jobs pay much. What can I say? My parents are still rebels in their way, still wanting to do things by their own rules.

I just showed these pages to Lorraine because he has been sitting next to me curious about what I'm writing. He said, not bad Kyle, your style is improving. It doesn't make me want to retch or anything. Then he went back to reading his book. It's some old book called *The Art of War*. The thing about Lorraine is he doesn't do anything without immersing himself into it. He wants to be a soldier, so he's going to find out about soldiering. No matter what you think about that, you have to admit that what I said about him from the beginning is true. He is an impressive individual.

Lorraine has been living with us since he found us in Toronto after the publicity about Granddad's troubles clued him in to the fact that we were living in Canada. He had been on the streets for a while, surviving by his wits, more or less. He found me and I took him home to Mom and Dad, who immediately tried to get a hold of his parents, but since he had not gone to the school they wanted him to go to, and he had used the network to get out of the country, they pretty much disowned him. So Mom and Dad let him live with us. It's been fun. It's like having a brother I never had. It was his idea to try this program. He said I needed to explore my propensity for violence and a program like this was just the thing. I would come to understand violence is a skill, and I would learn to keep it from controlling me. He also said I would come to understand what kind of person I truly was deep down inside: someone comfortable with violence, or someone who was fundamentally a pacifist who made a mistake or two. Mom was not happy about the idea, but she let me go. I can't make decisions for you forever, she said. At some point you are going to have to steer your own life. I think she believes I'll be so turned off by the soldiering that I won't even consider actually becoming a soldier.

The war with China has heated up some. There are more skirmishes, more deaths, more disruptions. I worry about Margolis but check her website periodically, and see she is still posting pictures, so she must be ok. Lorraine says she is an insanely brave person and he admires her courage and hopes she stays well. I can only agree.

The propaganda machine on both sides has ramped up to a high degree. Canada is still trying to stay out of the conflict, but it's becoming increasingly hard for it not to take sides. Lorraine says Canada will be sucked into a shooting war eventually. I find myself, perversely, almost hoping for it, because if the political climate changes, then they might not think my grandfather was so bad after all, and things might go better for him in his trial. But I know I can't depend on that happening. It is only a hope. Lorraine says we can't stay neutral forever and at some point Canada will have to take up arms alongside its long time ally. I don't know if he's right or wrong. This country has stayed out of other conflicts, but it has also been a part of some, so I guess time will tell.

For now, it just feels good to be going some place where there are trees. I still miss the woods around Cedar Falls. I think about the war, and how people's lives are turned around and upside down by war and it just makes me feel sad. But knowing there are woods somewhere, silent and abiding, fills me with joy. To think there are places untouched by the kind of senseless conflict that brings only misery, that thought gives me solace and hope that trusting in the future may not be a completely futile enterprise.

About the author

Mario Milosevic grew up in Northern Ontario and now lives in the Pacific Northwest of the United States. He has written novels for teens and adults, including *The Last Giant, The Coma Monologues,* and *Terrastina and Mazolli: a Novel in 99-word Episodes.* His collections of poetry include *Animal Life, Fantasy Life,* and *Love Life.* He is married to fellow writer Kim Antieau, and works at his local public library. Learn more at mariowrites.com.